Cinderellas in the Spotlight

Could their Prince Charmings be waiting under the mistletoe?

It all started so i............................ ...but what happ................................ ....tart of somethin......................................iend,

Because v......................... ...o the numbers for.................. ...ew Year's Eve party, a pretend midnight kiss with Celeste's delectable brother Damon feels anything but fake...!

Meanwhile next door, when Celeste clashes with TV quiz host Theo, she can't help but wonder if the sparks flying between them could mean something more than television banter...

What's clear is now is the time for these two heroines to stand in the spotlight while they discover they are worthy of meeting their perfect prince!

Awakening His Shy Cinderella

This Christmas, a shy, awkward Cinderella finally learns to ask for what she really wants—love, with her best friend's younger brother!

A Midnight Kiss to Seal the Deal

Can a pretend romance between two complete opposites lead to true love by the time Big Ben strikes midnight on New Year's Eve?

Dear Reader,

January 1 always feels like such a fresh start. A brand-new year, full of opportunities. But of course, in order to take advantage of them, we have to know what we want to do, where we want to go and who we want to be. How else can we choose the resolutions we want to make?

Celeste and Theo in this story have both still got a ways to go before they can do that—which is why it's a good thing the story starts on December 1. They've both spent their lives believing what other people said was true about them and following the paths set out before them. Now they've got one month to figure out who they really want to be on their own terms. But they're going to need each other to do to it. Do you think they'll manage it? Read on to find out.

To all my readers, I want to wish you a happy New Year, whenever you're reading this. I hope the next twelve months are filled with wonder and magic and romance!

Love and wishes,

Sophie x

A Midnight Kiss to Seal the Deal

Sophie Pembroke

◈ HARLEQUIN

Romance

HARLEQUIN®

Romance™

Recycling programs
for this product may
not exist in your area.

ISBN-13: 978-1-335-56682-9

A Midnight Kiss to Seal the Deal

Copyright © 2021 by Sophie Pembroke

This edition published by arrangement with Harlequin Books S.A.

For questions and comments about the quality of this book,
please contact us at CustomerService@Harlequin.com.

Harlequin Enterprises ULC
22 Adelaide St. West, 40th Floor
Toronto, Ontario M5H 4E3, Canada
www.Harlequin.com

Printed in U.S.A.

Sophie Pembroke has been dreaming, reading and writing romance ever since she read her first Harlequin novel as part of her English literature degree at Lancaster University, so getting to write romantic fiction for a living really is a dream come true! Born in Abu Dhabi, Sophie grew up in Wales and now lives in a little Hertfordshire market town with her scientist husband, her incredibly imaginative and creative daughter, and her adventurous, adorable little boy. In Sophie's world, happy *is* forever after, everything stops for tea and there's always time for one more page...

Visit the Author Profile page
at Harlequin.com for more titles.

To all the New Year's resolution makers out there

**Praise for
Sophie Pembroke**

"Wow, what an amazing story! Sophie Pembroke
made me fall in love with her characters in
Pregnant on the Earl's Doorstep from the get-go.
This book was such a fun, sweet, romantic
rendezvous! I got lost in the sway of emotions, the
tantalizing grip of romance and got swept away by
the visual detailing that is so well written."

—*Goodreads*

CHAPTER ONE

CELESTE HUNTER GRIPPED the phone in her hand a little tighter and whispered the words she'd never thought she'd say into it.

'What if I'm not good enough?'

On the other end of the line her agent, Richard, laughed. 'I don't believe it. Are you actually *nervous*?'

Celeste scowled, even though he obviously couldn't see her. 'Isn't that a perfectly natural response to appearing on television for the first time?'

'I didn't think you *had* natural responses, darling.' Richard sighed. She could just picture him shaking his head, his hand already hovering over his computer mouse as he moved on to more important things.

'I am human, you realise.'

'You're basically a walking encyclopaedia. Or history textbook, I guess.' She could hear his dismissive shrug. 'You're on a quiz show that

is quite literally called the *Christmas Cracker
Cranium Quiz*. I hardly think any of the questions are likely to stump you.'

'You're right.' Celeste knew she was intelligent. She'd had an excellent education and had
a phenomenal memory for detail. Those were
the things that had taken her as far as she'd gone
in her academic career so far. She was a great
historian.

That wasn't the part she was worried about.

'You're thinking about the new show,' Richard guessed, correctly.

'*Possible* new show,' she corrected him. The
TV show they'd pitched for was very much still
at the discussions stage, and Celeste just knew
that the production company would be watching her appearance on the quiz to decide if she
really had what it took to front a history show
by herself. 'No counting chickens, remember?'

'Where does that saying come from, anyway?'

'Aesop,' Celeste answered absently.

'See! You know everything!' Richard yelled
gleefully. 'Now stop worrying. I have to go deal
with an actress with a secret lovechild with a
politician. *That's* real problems.'

Celeste laughed. 'Good luck with that.'

'And you break a leg on that show, you hear
me?' He paused, just for a second. 'But not lit-

erally. You know that, right? It's just a saying. Like the chickens.'

'I know that.' Poor Richard. He still hadn't quite adjusted to having an academic for a client, rather than actresses and pop stars. She'd never been entirely sure what had made him take her on in the first place—she didn't think he was, either. Curiosity, maybe. Or boredom.

Whatever, it seemed to be working out so far.

'Seriously, Celeste. Go sit in the green room with your laptop, and work on that book of yours. Not the academic treatise on whatever it was. The fun one. The popular one.'

'Two things I've never been in my life,' Celeste joked, but even she could hear the edge to it.

'That's what you're worrying about?' Richard sighed again. He was a big guy, in his late fifties, with a bushy beard that was more salt than pepper. When he sighed, his whole body moved, like a sad-faced dog. Even though she couldn't see him, just imagining it made Celeste feel a little better.

'If Tim and Fiona from the production company watch this…what if they decide I'm not enough? That I don't have…whatever it takes to be *good* at this.' That elusive X factor, she supposed.

'Have you ever *not* been good at something before?' Richard asked.

'Not really.' Apart from making friends and not boring people. Her best friend, Rachel, was the solitary exception to the rule. Even her brother, Damon, who she was pretty sure at least loved her, found her dull, she was sure. And her parents…well. They were pleased by her academic successes anyway. She hoped.

They certainly weren't pleased by any of her media successes. Apparently, she was *'dumbing down important research until all you have to say is derivative and reductive'.*

'Then have faith that you'll be good at this, too. Theo Montgomery's hosting, yeah? Follow his lead if you feel lost. He's good at charming a room, whatever the papers are saying about him at the moment.'

Celeste pulled a face. She didn't know what the papers were saying particularly, but she knew of Theo Montgomery. The sort of guy who got where he was because of his name, his face, and surface charm—but nothing underneath it. No substance.

Whereas she was nothing *but* substance.

Yeah, she really couldn't see Theo Montgomery being her new role model, whatever Richard thought.

Sighing, Celeste looked down at the Christmas jumper the wardrobe department had forced her into—worlds away from her usual, safe black outfits. Maybe that was the trick—to pretend this wasn't her here at all. She could be TV Celeste, instead of University Celeste.

Except she'd never really been very good at pretending to be something she wasn't.

Perhaps it was time to learn. If she wanted that show…

And she did. She couldn't explain why—especially not to her academic parents, who would be horrified she was contemplating something so…pedestrian. But she loved teaching history at the university, loved sharing her knowledge about her specialist area—women in classical literature and ancient history. And the idea of spreading that knowledge further, of getting people who might never have even thought about the subject before excited about those historical and mythical figures she loved, that excited her.

She just wasn't sure that she was the right person to do it.

'You're right. I'll go work on the book.' Working—whether it was researching or writing or teaching—always calmed her down. She knew what she was doing there.

It was only outside that safe world where she had all the answers that she struggled.

'Good. And, Celeste?' Richard said. 'Try to smile, yeah?'

Celeste scowled again, an automatic response to being asked to smile, honed after years of men telling her how much prettier she'd be if she did. And then she hung up, since her agent was clearly out of useful information.

She was just going to have to do this her own way. Starting with mentally preparing herself by focussing on something she *knew* she was good at. Writing her book.

And woe betide anyone who interrupted her.

Theo Montgomery was on a mission. Or a dare. A bet, perhaps. No, mission sounded better. More exciting, yes. But also more…official. As if it gave him a reason for being there, sneaking around the green room instead of hanging out in his private dressing room as he normally would for a show like this.

And there had been a lot of shows like this. Well, not *exactly* the same—the *Christmas Cracker Cranium Quiz* was definitely a one-off. But he'd presented a lot of special occasion quiz shows, or entertainment specials. Apparently his was the face the network liked to trot out for this kind of thing.

He wasn't going to complain about that—especially right now. He knew that, after everything that had been published about him in the papers lately, he was lucky to still have the show. Even if it might be nice, every now and again, to be wanted for something other than his face, or his family name, Theo was under no illusions that the combination of both were what had got him where he was—TV darling, never short of work, or a date, or someone asking for his autograph.

Or where he'd been, before this mess of a break-up with Tania that was all anyone seemed to be talking about lately.

But overall, he had what he'd always wanted. What his family wanted for him, after a fashion. And he wasn't so bloody ungrateful as to complain about it now. Not when he had a lot of viewers to bring back on side, too. Viewers who'd listened to Tania's side of the story and jumped to the wrong conclusions.

The break-up had been amicable enough, Theo had thought. They hadn't even been together all that long. But the British press had loved the whole alliterative relationship, Tania and Theo, the reality TV star and the presenter, so they'd earned a lot of column inches.

And Tania had been a lot happier to tell her side of the break-up—with embellishments— than he had.

His agent, Cerys, had made it clear they

were on a mission to salvage his career now. It was hard to be the nation's sweetheart when the same nation was tutting at him and saying 'that poor girl' behind his back.

Or, as Cerys put it, *'They want to be wooed, Theo. Charm them back onto your side again. Remind them why they love you.'*

So Theo would smile, and be charming, and ask the questions and laugh at the poor jokes attempted by the semi-famous contestants, and hint at the answers when they got stuck because it was *Christmas*, and nobody really took this sort of quiz seriously, right?

And talking of the contestants, that brought him right back to his current mission.

Because this was supposed to be a 'cranium quiz,' something a little harder than the usual *Who was Christmas number one in 1989?*— 'Do They Know It's Christmas?' of course—the producers had also trotted out a higher intellectual calibre of celebrity guests.

There was the astrophysicist who did all the shows about the solar system, the kids' presenter who made Shakespeare accessible for primary school children, the morning TV doctor who treated the nation's bunions and STDs, the mathematician from that other quiz show, the guitarist from that band who also had a PhD in psychology and, last of all, the rising-star historian, an academic who was starting to make a name for herself, bringing the ancient world to life in guest slots on radio show interview and history podcasts.

Everyone except the historian he'd met on things like this before, or at some party or another after an awards ceremony. He'd actually been clubbing with the kids' TV presenter, David, while the guy was still in Shakespearean dress. And he and the mathematician, Lucy, had even had a bit of a thing, for a few nights, a couple of years ago.

No, his mission didn't involve any of them. It was centred firmly on the historian.

Celeste Hunter.

Before the show started, he was going to find her, introduce himself, maybe even charm her a little. Because he was pretty sure that Celeste Hunter was someone he was going to want to get to know.

He might not have met her, but that didn't mean he wasn't aware of her. He'd heard her speaking on plenty of podcasts and radio shows over the last few months, in that way that often happened in the media. Rumour had it she was lined up for her own series, soon. Once a person got a little bit of attention from one show, suddenly they were everywhere.

Like him.

And in this case, Theo thought it was a good thing. Celeste Hunter was *interesting*. Engaging, even, when talking about subjects that mattered to her—like ancient history.

But she wasn't just a specialist, he knew. He'd heard her talk about periods of history throughout the ages. She was a *brilliant* addition to today's quiz, and he was a genius for suggesting her to the producers. They'd joke about history, riff off some of the questions, and she'd make him look really good again for the cameras. Because, although no one would guess from his public profile, Theo liked history. He even knew a bit about it—although nowhere near as much as Celeste. He was interested though and engaged—and, knowing there was a fair smattering of historical questions in the stack for Celeste, he was most excited about that part of the show.

Theo eased his way into the green room, past an assistant carrying a tray of coffees, and smiled at the various inhabitants. There was so much festive filming going on in the building today that all the contestants had been shoved together in one of the green rooms, after hair and make-up. Luckily they all seemed in good enough spirits about it.

He greeted all the celebrities he knew, exchanging quick pleasantries and jokes, and even a hug with Lucy the mathematician.

'It's so great that you could all be here for this today,' he said, filling the words with his trademark enthusiasm. 'I really think this is going to be a "cracker" of a show.'

There were good-humoured groans at that, and he flashed them all a smile before turning to find the one person in the room he didn't know already.

She was sitting at the other end of the green room, as far away from everyone else as it was possible to get. He'd only ever heard her on the radio, but Theo had to admit his first look at Celeste Hunter didn't quite match up to his imagination.

She'd sounded so self-assured, so confident on the radio, he'd assumed she'd be older—older than him, at least. But the slender, serious woman tapping away on her laptop in the corner looked younger than him, if anything. Her dark hair was artfully waved around her face, something he assumed Sandra in Hair and Make-up was responsible for, given the way Celeste kept pushing it out of her eyes in irritation. She was wearing black jeans and heeled boots, her ankles crossed in front of her as she stretched out her long legs, the laptop resting on her knees. The jeans were paired with a sparkly festive jumper that he thought might actually light up, given the dimmed bulbs dotted around the Christmas tree design. It was so at odds with her serious, concentrated face, it made him smile as he approached, moving into her space and waiting for her to notice him there.

It took about a minute longer than it usually would.

Finally, Celeste Hunter tapped a last key on her laptop, looked up at him, and scowled. 'Can I help you?' She didn't sound as if she wanted to help him. Maybe he shouldn't have interrupted her work.

'Hi there! I'm Theo Montgomery, the host of today's show.' He gave her his most charming smile, and hoped for the best.

'Yes.' Her gaze flicked back to her computer screen, then up to him again.

Right. 'Since you're the only contestant today I haven't met before, I thought I'd come and introduce myself.' Like a normal, friendly person.

This usually worked a lot better than this.

She stared at him. 'Okay. Do you need me to introduce myself too?'

She sounded reluctant. Theo took a seat beside her anyway. 'You're Celeste Hunter. I liked your piece on the Roman Empire in Britain on the radio last week.'

That earned him a surprised look, but a scowl

soon settled back across her face, as she looked back at her screen. 'Apparently it was derivative and reductive.'

He didn't contradict her, even though he hadn't thought that at all. His opinion wouldn't matter to her, he guessed, and even on five minutes' acquaintance he was sure she wouldn't hesitate to tell him so. He had enough experience of being told that his job was meaningless or didn't qualify him to talk on any subject except charming people. He suspected Celeste would say the same about him, and he couldn't imagine that tonight's quiz was going to change that.

Shame. This was one guest he'd actually been looking forward to meeting, had lobbied to have included because he'd assumed she'd be as fascinating and engaging in real life as she was when presenting on the radio. He'd hoped he'd be able to talk to her about his own interest in history, his own studies and hopes to move more into that sphere.

Apparently not. This was why people should never meet their heroes.

Theo got to his feet, fairly sure Celeste wouldn't notice or care if he just left now. Still, the good manners his mother had ingrained in him long before his agent had insisted on them meant that he couldn't just walk away. So he smiled, and said, 'Well, I'd better go and get ready—we'll be starting filming soon. I'll see you out there. Break a leg!'

Celeste winced at his words, then nodded at him in acknowledgment, before beginning to type again.

Right, then. Clearly not a people person—which was a shame, since apparently charming people was the only thing Theo was qualified to do. Celeste Hunter was uncharmable, though, it seemed.

Which was fine. After all, once they got through filming tonight's show, he'd never have to see her again anyway.

Whistling to himself, Theo waved goodbye to the other guests and headed back to his dressing room to perform his traditional pre-show routine.

This was going to be a great show, a great night, and Celeste Hunter wasn't going to ruin that for him.

Where the hell are Damon and Rachel?

Celeste paced the corridor outside the green room, waiting for her brother and best friend to *finally* show up. She'd tried working on her manuscript to distract her from her growing nerves and her mother's voice in her head, telling her that this show was an insult to her PhD, but then Theo Montgomery had interrupted her with that charming TV-star smile, and reminded her all over again that this sort of show was *not* what she'd studied all these years to do.

God, her parents were going to be so disappointed when they found out about this. A TV series of her own, she might have just about been able to swing. Well, probably not, but she could dream... The *Christmas Cracker Cranium Quiz*? No. She'd tried mentioning it before, in rather vague terms, but the look on her mother's face had stopped her even considering going into details.

Normal parents would be excited for her. Proud, even. But then Jacob and Diana Hunter had never pretended to be normal. Never wanted to be, either.

Which was why she needed Damon and Rachel to just *get here*. They were normal people. They'd remind her that, actually, this was fun and festive and a boost to her career. The chance to show that production company that she had what it took to front her own show. It was the kind of opportunity most people would be hugely grateful for, even if she had no idea who at the network had dredged her name out of the halls of academia to take part.

She had a feeling it wouldn't happen again, not after that moment in the green room.

She'd been rude to Theo Montgomery. She hadn't *meant* to be, exactly. She just didn't deal with interruptions well. And since she'd already been freaking out a little bit about the company she was keeping in there—people her *parents* would probably recognise, and they didn't even own a television—well, she'd sort of just reacted, without thinking about it. Damon had been trying to break her of that habit for most of his life, but it never seemed to take.

She should probably apologise. Later.

First, she needed to get through the filming.

Celeste had never done anything like this before. Radio, sure, where she just had to answer a few questions she definitely knew the answers to—that was why they asked her to come on the show, because she knew about it. They were always pre-recorded, and usually she had an idea of the questions the presenter was going to ask before she even showed up, so she could prepare.

She liked being prepared.

But this…as she'd looked around the green room it had been obvious that this was a general knowledge quiz, ranging from science and maths to literature and arts, and hopefully history somewhere in between. She would be expected to know things *outside* her area of expertise.

The exact opposite of what she'd been training for her whole life.

'*You have to specialise, Celeste,*' her parents had been telling her, ever since she was in her teens. '*If you don't know exactly what matters to you, then you won't matter at all. Generalists never get anywhere. You need to find a niche, squat in it, and defend it with your life.*'

Her parents were academics. She'd wanted to be an academic. Of course, she'd listened to them.

Her brother, Damon, meanwhile, had rebelled, gone completely the opposite way, and become the quintessential Jack of all trades. While she had settled into her niche—women in the ancient world—and only dabbled in other areas of historical research as a bit of a hobby.

A well-rounded view of world history was generally encouraged in the Hunter household. A well-rounded view of anything else was generally not.

And appearing on a Christmas quiz show that reduced human knowledge to questions about Christmas number ones was *definitely* frowned upon.

She'd swotted up on a lot of festive history, ready for the occasion, though. Just in case.

'We'll be starting soon, Ms Hunter,' a production assistant told her as she hurried past.

Celeste's heartbeat jumped, and she fumbled for her phone in her pocket. She needed to remember to switch it off. Or leave it in the green room, probably.

But first… She hit autodial for her last number and tapped her foot impatiently as it rang and rang.

'Where are you?' Celeste asked, as soon as her best friend, Rachel, answered. 'We're starting filming any minute!'

'We're here, we're here,' Rachel replied soothingly. But Celeste could hear a car door opening, which suggested they weren't, actually, inside the building or anything. 'We'll be there any second now, I promise.'

'Okay. Hurry!' She hung up. Hopefully that was Rachel getting *out* of the car, rather than into it, or they'd never make it. And Celeste wasn't at all sure she could do this without them. Actually, she wasn't sure she could do it *with* them there, either, but the odds seemed slightly better, so she was going with it.

Three endless minutes later, Damon and Rachel tumbled through the doors into the lobby, and Celeste's whole body seemed to sway with relief. Only for a moment, though, because really they were very late.

'What took you so long?' she asked, grabbing Rachel's arm and pulling her into step with her.

'Let me guess, Damon was flirting with your stepsisters?' She should have predicted that. Allowed time for it. Historically, adding extra time to any schedule to compensate for Damon flirting was never a bad idea.

'Actually, it was my fault. I had to fix a window display before we left.' Rachel sounded apologetic, and Celeste felt briefly guilty for being so cross. She was sure that Rachel's stepmother would have been the one nagging her to fix it. For reasons Celeste only kind of understood, Rachel was reluctant to break the fragile peace that existed in her family, so of course she'd have risked being late to make her stepmother happy.

She still reckoned that Damon would have been flirting with Rachel's stepsisters in the meantime.

'Are you ready?' Damon asked, all charm and confidence and totally at ease with himself, as usual. How her little brother had got *all* the charm in the family, Celeste wasn't sure, but it did seem rather unfair. He always joked that it was because she got all the brains, but his highly successful business argued otherwise.

'Not really,' she admitted.

But it was too late. It was showtime, and there was already a production assistant hurrying down the corridor towards them ready to usher Celeste onto the set, while Damon and Rachel slipped into the audience.

'Break a leg,' Rachel whispered to her as they headed for their seats.

'Hopefully not,' Celeste muttered to herself. But she felt better for knowing that Damon and Rachel were out there anyway.

This would be fine.

CHAPTER TWO

THIS WAS HORRENDOUS.

Maybe if Theo broke some sort of minor bone he could get out of doing the rest of the show. There was bound to be someone else in the building who'd be happy to take over from him. Let *them* deal with the quiz show guest from hell. Because he was pretty sure this festive televisual outing was going to do nothing to repair his fractured reputation.

As Celeste explained—not for the first time—why the answer card he'd been given was actually inaccurate, Theo could see the producer, Derek, glaring at him from just off set. Damn. Apparently, Derek remembered exactly whose idea it had been to invite Celeste on the show in the first place. He'd been kind of hoping everyone would have forgotten about that.

The worst part was, under other circumstances, the stuff she was saying would be interesting. And she was passionate and engaged as she talked about it—far more than she had been during that awkward meeting in the green room. Theo found he genuinely wanted to know more about why the story about Prince Albert bringing Christmas trees to Britain from Germany was wrong. Just…not right now. Not in front of a studio audience that was clearly getting more uncomfortable by the second. Not when they had to finish another three rounds of this damn quiz, and the other celebrity contestants were getting restless.

Had she finished? He thought she might have done. To be honest, he'd stopped listening, and focussed instead on his inner panic about his career circling the drain.

Theo grabbed the next card from the pile and prayed that it would be about anything other than history. Thank God, children's literature. That should buy him a minute or two. He was sure there was a question in the stack somewhere about who sent the first ever Christmas card, and he had a feeling the answer was going to be wrong.

Had she been reading up about festive history, ready for tonight? She must have been.

'Move it along, Theo,' the impatient voice came in his ear, and he tried to focus on the words on the card.

'In your teams now, can you name all eight

of the reindeer that feature in the classic Christmas story, *The Night Before Christmas*?' That should be safe enough, right? For starters, Celeste wasn't a team captain. David would have to give the answer to this one. And then it was the end of the round, and Theo was pretty sure they would call a break after that. They'd been at this for hours longer than they should have been already.

David buzzed and gave the correct answer, while Celeste sat silent beside him. Had she even weighed in on that question? Theo didn't think so. Obviously, she didn't know *absolutely* everything, then. That was kind of reassuring.

A break was called, and Theo jumped out from behind the presenter's desk, desperate to move. He'd never been good at staying still, one of the reasons he'd rejected any kind of office job as a career option. He needed variety, and the ability to wander about and chat to people.

He veered left, away from the production team, though, when he realised they were in a serious-looking huddle, presumably discussing this disaster of a show. The rest of the contestants similarly had gathered around the red team's side, leaving Celeste sitting alone behind her team's desk.

Theo sighed. This kind of was his fault. He'd suggested bringing her in when, clearly, this wasn't a good fit for her. She must be hating every minute.

He'd never been any good at letting a situation fester—not at work, anyway—so he moved towards her, ignoring the part of his brain that told him that, on past evidence, this was a stupid idea. She looked up as he approached, and Theo could see the resignation settle on her face.

'Hey, how are you doing? Do you need more water?' The jug in front of her was full, and Celeste just gave it a pointed look before returning her gaze to meet his, with a slight smile.

It was a disturbingly direct gaze, and Theo shifted uncomfortably under it. There was none of the charmed expression and delightedness he usually tried to inspire in people in that smile.

Celeste Hunter's eyes said, *I am here, you are here, why is this?* And nothing more.

Theo bit the inside of his cheek to stop himself automatically confessing all the reasons for his existence and—more pertinently—her presence on his quiz show.

'Did you need something?' Celeste asked, eventually, having obviously concluded that he was too stupid to continue this conversation on his own after his ridiculous water statement.

'I just wanted to see how…how you thought this was going.' Over Celeste's shoulder, he could see the production team watching him. He was pretty sure the other contestants would be doing the same behind him. All waiting to see if she was about to tear him to shreds again.

'I think your question team need to be a little more thorough in their research,' she said, folding her hands neatly on the table in front of her. 'But otherwise, fine.'

Fine. She thought this was fine. 'Have you ever actually seen a TV quiz show?' The words were out of his mouth before he could stop them, and he heard an audible gasp from Lucy the mathematician.

Celeste's expression didn't change. Her hands didn't move. She was completely and utterly still and in control.

'Of course, I have. Well, once or twice. Maybe just once, start to finish. They weren't exactly required viewing for my PhD. But I did my research and watched *you* on some of those shows. Clips of you anyway.' She tilted her head to study him. 'Your face is less shiny on TV.'

His face was less shiny when he wasn't so stressed.

'Why did you agree to do this show?' he asked desperately. He couldn't be the only one to blame here, right? Yes, he'd suggested she take part. But *she'd* agreed.

'I wanted to…' For the first time, she flinched, and looked away. 'My agent thought it was a good idea. He said it would build my profile.'

Of course. Even if Celeste clearly had no showbiz instincts, her agent would. He wondered if the poor guy was sitting out there watching, seeing all his dreams of discovering the next big docu-star going up in the smoke coming out of Celeste's ears as she argued with the answer card.

Come to that, he hoped his own agent wasn't out there tonight. She hadn't said she'd be coming, had she? He'd rather delay the inevitable tongue-lashing until after the thing had been aired.

He glanced out towards the audience and frowned. Was it less full out there than it had been before? He turned to the door and saw a queue of people leaving the studio. Surely it hadn't been that bad?

'Hang on a minute,' he said to Celeste, and crossed the set in a few long steps, collaring a young production assistant called Amy, who coloured prettily when he asked what was going on.

'They're needed in another studio,' she replied.

'There's another show *stealing* my audience?' He tried to sound outraged, but it came out rather more petulant, he thought. Damn, he was tired.

Amy glanced towards where Celeste was now disagreeing with David, her team captain, about something. 'To be honest, I'm pretty sure they all went willingly.'

Theo sighed as the studio doors closed and the call went up to resume filming. 'I don't blame them. Come on, let's get this over with.'

Oh, that had been horrible. Whose idea had this been anyway? Why on earth had she ever thought that she could do a show like this anyway? She wasn't built for it. She couldn't smile prettily or charm people as Theo could. She could educate them, correct them. But make them like her? No.

She was never going to get her TV show after this. But what else was she supposed to do? This was who she was.

Okay, maybe she hadn't needed to get into that argument with Theo about who sent the first Christmas card. And she probably shouldn't have told him his face was shiny; TV guys were sensitive about that sort of thing, right? But in truth, she'd been flustered. And nervous. And lots of other things she wasn't used to being.

In her confined, academic world, she was in control. She could be calm, collected and sure, safe in her knowledge and her education. Out here in the showbiz world…not so much.

There had just been so much she *didn't* know. Oh, not so much the specialist stuff, where the questions had clearly been put in to cater to individual contestants' knowledge base. She didn't care about them; they weren't her speciality, why should she know the answers?

It was the general, everyday Christmas knowledge that got to her. Like the quick-fire round at the end, all about silly Christmas traditions that everyone was clamouring to answer because they were so easy.

She'd hardly known any of them. And the ones she did, she'd only learned from watching TV with Rachel.

Her family had their own, unique traditions, she supposed. Just another way that they weren't like everyone else. Her parents had always implied it made them superior, in some way. But right now, Celeste wasn't so sure.

The other contestants had all left by now—she'd heard them talking about going to a bar together afterwards, but she hadn't been invited. Not that she'd have gone if she had. The crew were clearing up and the audience filing out—a lot fewer of them than there had been, Celeste admitted. The filming had gone on much longer than planned.

She supposed that was probably her fault.

No, not just her fault. Theo Montgomery's

fault, too. He was the one who had kept arguing back at her, who couldn't accept that she was *right*. She knew history. It was the one thing she *did* know. So why wouldn't he let her tell him he was wrong?

Maybe he was just one of those men who had to be right all the time. Like her father.

There was no sign of Damon and Rachel in the thinning audience so, figuring that the coast was probably clear by now, Celeste headed back to the green room to gather her things, changed out of the miserably sparkly light-up Christmas jumper and handed it back to the wardrobe people. Then, resigned to chalking the whole TV thing up to experience and never trying it again, she headed out to find her missing brother and best friend.

The first half of that proved to be easier than she'd expected: Damon was waiting for her in the corridor outside the green room. Celeste tried not to show how relieved she felt to see a friendly face.

She and Damon might be as different as siblings could be, but he *knew* her. Understood her, at least more than most people.

Celeste didn't have many people in her life who mattered to her, but Damon and Rachel were the heart of them.

She showed her love by scowling at her brother and stomping towards him.

'Where on earth did you go? And where's Rachel?'

Damon's easy smile made her feel a little less stressed, at least. 'We got dragged in to film this New Year party show. They didn't have enough partygoers because of some issue on the Tube, and your filming had already gone on longer than it was supposed to anyway.' Of course they had. Because wherever Damon went, he always found the coolest room to be in, the best party to attend. And it was never the same one that Celeste was in.

Celeste rolled her eyes as she pushed past him to continue stomping down the corridor and decided to focus on the second part of his statement. Yes, the filming had run long. But it wasn't *her* fault. 'Only because *that man* kept getting things wrong.'

She didn't need to look back to know that Damon was laughing at her. Silently, but still laughing. 'In fairness, Theo Montgomery was only reading out the answers on the cards.'

'Because he's not bright enough to actually know anything himself,' Celeste shot back over her shoulder. Then she winced and felt the colour flooding to her cheeks as she saw the man emerging from the room behind Damon into the corridor.

Theo Montgomery, of course. And from his raised eyebrows, he'd heard everything Celeste said.

She hadn't meant it, not really. She was just off kilter, and that made her defensive. Damon knew that, because he knew her. Theo didn't.

Damon stepped towards him, hand out for Theo to shake, which he did. Because he was a nice guy, like her brother, who knew how to be polite and charming in a way Celeste was never going to manage.

'Mr Montgomery. I'm Damon Hunter, Celeste's brother—we met earlier? I just wanted to take this opportunity to apologise for my sister.'

Great. Rub it in. Yes, I'm rubbish with people and you're not.

Why did she like her brother, again?

'No need,' Theo said, just as jovially. 'Trust me, I've heard worse. You stayed for the whole filming?' He sounded amazed at the prospect. Celeste didn't blame him.

Damon shook his head. 'No, I just follow my sister around to make the necessary apologies. And now that's done, I'm heading home.'

Wait. They couldn't go home. Because they were still missing someone. Celeste might not have the interpersonal skills of her brother, but at least she kept track of her best friend. The people that mattered to her, Celeste understood and cared for.

Everyone else…not so much.

'Where's Rachel?' Celeste asked again, ignoring Theo. 'I said we'd give her a lift home.'

'She, uh…she left early,' Damon said.

Okay, that was a lie. If her brother knew her, she knew him too, and she knew when he was lying. Besides, he sounded guilty as hell.

Celeste narrowed her eyes. 'What did you do?'

'What makes you think I did anything?' He turned to Theo. 'Does it make you feel any better that she treats *everyone* this way?' he asked, as if she weren't there at all.

'A little,' Theo admitted. Celeste continued ignoring him.

'You always do something,' she said to Damon, instead. 'Let me guess, you were flirting with some other woman at the bar and leaving her all on her own?'

'I can promise you that absolutely was not the case. I was attentive, friendly, we even danced together.'

'Rachel *danced*?' Well, that was a red flag if anything was. 'I have never once, in ten full years, seen my best friend dance. There is something else going on here, and you are going to tell me all about it on the way home. Come on, let's get to the car.' Then, suddenly remembering his existence, she turned to Theo. 'Thank you for having me on your show, Mr Montgomery. I'm very sorry that the question team screwed up so many of your answer cards.' Okay, it probably wasn't exactly what the etiquette guides would recommend, but she'd made an effort. That counted for something, right?

'Once again, apologies for my sister's attempt at an apology,' she heard Damon saying as she walked away.

She was out of earshot before Theo replied, which she decided was probably for the best.

'Did you skip the year at school where everyone else learned how to make friends?' Damon asked as Celeste settled into the heated front seat of his overly fancy car.

'Actually, yes.' Her parents had insisted that she be put up a year, since her birthday was so early in the year anyway, and she'd already known everything they'd be teaching her in reception. Until recently, that had always been a point of pride for her.

Suddenly, she wasn't quite so sure it should be.

Damon rolled his eyes and started the engine.

'Right, of course you did. Well, maybe it's time for some sort of catch-up lesson. Starting with, if you want to make friends you have to actually let people in, rather than automatically pushing them away.'

'I don't know what you're talking about.' She crossed her arms over her chest, happy to be back in her own plain black V-neck sweater again. Sparkly festive-wear was really not her thing.

'Did Theo Montgomery try to be nice to you?' Damon asked patiently.

'Maybe.' She supposed that was what he'd been doing when he'd interrupted her in the green room. At the time, she'd only registered that he'd disturbed her work and heightened her nervousness, not why he'd been doing it.

'Was he, in fact, friendly?' Damon pushed. 'Because he seemed like a friendly guy to me.'

'I suppose.' Celeste scowled out of the car window. 'What does it matter now? I never have to see the guy again.'

Damon sighed. 'Call it a lesson for next time. When someone is pleasant to you, try being pleasant back. You might actually make a friend. Or something more.'

'You're assuming that I want more friends,' Celeste pointed out, ignoring the pang inside her chest at the idea. Yes, maybe she sometimes wished she were better with people, as Damon was. And yes, it would be nice to meet someone. Someone special. But that wasn't how her life went. She'd accepted that long before now. 'I have too much research to do—and a whole book to write—to have time to spend with new friends. Besides, I have Rachel.'

'Yes, you do,' Damon said, his voice suddenly soft as he spoke about her best friend.

Celeste turned to study his face in the glow of the streetlights they passed. Yep, there was definitely something going on there.

'What really happened with Rachel tonight?'

'I told you.' Damon reached out and pressed the button to turn on the radio, and a Christmas number one from before she was born filled the car. 'Nothing happened.'

He was lying. But then, so was she.

So Celeste let it go. For now.

Four days later, Theo woke up too early on Saturday morning to his phone buzzing. And buzzing. And buzzing, until it buzzed its way off the bedside table and crashed onto the floor.

He lay back, buried in the pillow, listening to it vibrate against the hardwood floor of his London flat, and weighed up the merits of ignoring it against answering it.

On the one hand, his phone lighting up

the moment his do-not-disturb ended at—he squinted at the clock—six-thirty in the morning had never yet turned out to mean anything good. On the other, he wasn't going to get any more sleep with this racket going on, and his downstairs neighbours would be banging on the ceiling soon if he didn't stop it. His apartment building might be in one of the most expensive areas of London, and security was excellent, but someone had definitely skimped on the sound-proofing.

The phone stopped. Theo held his breath.

Buzz.

He sighed as the device began its journey across the floor again, powered only by its own vibrations. Then he swung his legs out of bed, swooped down and picked it up.

'Hello?' He suspected that there were a hundred notifications waiting for him, from the way it had been behaving, but right now the immediate call was his priority. Especially as the caller ID read Lord And Master, after the caller had nabbed his phone in the pub one night and changed it. He really should change that back some time.

'Where the hell have you been?' Cerys, his long-term agent, snapped the moment he answered.

'Sleeping. Like normal people. It's the weekend, Cerys.' He forced a loud yawn, just to prove the point.

'Theo, you forget that I know you're not actually the lazy, artless aristocrat you pretend to be. So quit acting with me and pay attention.'

Damn. With anyone else he would have got away with that. People saw what they expected to see, in Theo's experience. And when they looked at him they saw someone who had all the advantages of life, all the education, money, looks and privilege it was possible to have, and used it to entertain people on telly on a Saturday night. So they expected him to be equally frivolous with his brain, his time, his money, his life.

In a lot of ways, they weren't wrong.

In others…well. Theo hoped he'd prove them at least premature in their judgement, eventually.

But not Cerys. Cerys knew exactly who he was, what his ambitions were and how damn hard he worked to get there. Which meant there was no fooling Cerys.

And since he was already in her bad books for the whole Tania mess, he'd better play nice.

'What's happened?' he asked, sitting up a little straighter, and reaching for the tablet on his bedside table. Despite being in silent mode, it was managing to convey a sense of dramatic urgency through constantly flashing notifications from every social media or news site he'd ever signed up to.

'Did you watch the show when it aired last night?' Cerys asked, sounding calmer, at least.

'The *Christmas Cracker Cranium Quiz*?' Theo enunciated carefully; that name was a total tongue-twister, one he almost suspected the producers of coming up with as punishment for him for something, as he'd had to say it repeatedly through the show. Maybe one of them was friends with Tania. That would explain a lot.

'I don't know, Theo, did you spend twenty minutes mansplaining festive history to an actual *historian* on any other show this week?' Cerys snapped.

'What?' That wasn't what had happened. Was it? Theo ran through the filming again in his head. Celeste had argued with all of the history questions, of course, but that was just a small segment of the show. And he'd just explained what he'd had written on the answer cards...

Or *mansplained*. Apparently.

'I didn't—' he started, searching for a defence, but Cerys cut him off before he had time to find one anyway.

'I've seen the show, genius. Whatever you think happened isn't what the great British public watched last night, and that's all that really matters. *As you already know!*'

Theo winced. 'I need to watch it.'

'Yes. And while you're watching it, you need to read what everyone else who watched it is saying about it. About you.'

'I'm not going to like that part at all, am I?'

'Not even a little bit.' Cerys was a great agent, but she didn't believe in all that 'babying the client along' nonsense. They'd known each other too long anyway, Theo reasoned. If she suddenly started being nice to him, he'd know his career was over. 'You thought the Tania stuff was bad? This is worse. That was just you being an arsehole over a personal break-up—'

'I told you, it was amicable!' he interrupted.

Cerys ignored him. 'This is you being a patronising, superior arse on prime-time television.'

He hadn't been. Had he?

Theo shook his head. Cerys was right: it didn't matter what had actually happened. It mattered what the viewers *thought* had happened. He'd definitely learned that since the split with Tania.

Since Cerys was still being blunt and shouting at him, there must be a way out of this mess.

Travel back in time and not suggest Celeste Hunter as a guest on the quiz? Or just erase all knowledge of Celeste Hunter from my brain?

Hopefully a more practical way than anything he could come up with right now.

'Okay. I'll watch the show. I'll read the comments. And then what do I do?' he asked plaintively.

Cerys paused. Oh, that wasn't a good sign. Not at all.

'Cerys?'

'Shh. I'm thinking.'

Theo sat in anxious silence, willing his own brain to give him the answers. But then, he'd never been employed for his brain, had he? And even if he had, this kind of problem required the sort of strategic thinking that he'd never been good at.

That was why he'd hired Cerys.

As the silence stretched on Theo allowed himself to glance at the notifications on his tablet, taking in just the first lines of the many, many comments about him as they filled the screen.

Nation's sweetheart or nation's misogynist?

God, typical man. Has to be right about everything.

Privilege on show.

Well, of course he went to Eton, didn't he? So he thinks he knows everything.

It wasn't worth pointing out that he'd actually gone to Winchester, Theo knew. He put the tablet aside, although he was itching to read more—and to watch the actual show. Because as far as he remembered, he *hadn't* pretended to know better than Celeste. Because he didn't. Obviously. At least, not when it came to history.

He'd just had to give her the actual answer that was written on the card, as the director had been telling him to through his earpiece.

Had something happened in the editing room to make him appear a total arse? Or had he been more arsey in the first place than he'd ever realised? He wouldn't know until he watched it back.

God, he hated watching himself on television.

'Okay, here's what we're going to do,' Cerys said suddenly, and he tuned back into the phone call. 'We need to fix this—and quickly. Your reputation was battered enough before now; this really won't have helped. I don't think the Powers That Be will be planning on making any panicked changes before New Year, but we don't want to take that chance.'

'You mean, before I present the *New Year's Eve Spectacular*.' Live, in Central London, the biggest event of his career so far. The last thing he needed was protestors showing up to shout insults up at him or throw tomatoes or whatever. Or even just fewer people tuning in than normal to watch it in the first place, because he was presenting.

Or the Powers That Be deciding not to take the risk and instructing him to come down with a strategic case of laryngitis before December the thirty-first, so someone else could take his place.

Television was a precarious career, he'd always known that. But until now, he'd never realised quite how easy it was to slip and tumble down the slope from the top.

Cerys had always assumed it would be a sex scandal that would bring him down. So far, he was in trouble for *not* wanting to have sex with Tania any more, and for arguing about history. She must be so disappointed.

'Exactly,' was all she said. 'We need to fix this before anyone starts talking about making any changes. So right now, I'm going to make some phone calls, and get a number for you. While I'm doing that, you watch the show.'

'And then?'

'Then I'm going to call you back, give you that phone number, and you are going to follow my instructions *to the letter*. Okay?'

'Yes, ma'am,' Theo answered. Because although he already knew he wasn't going to like whatever Cerys's plan was, he liked the idea of losing his career even less.

CHAPTER THREE

Have you watched this yet? Call me when you have.

THE INNOCUOUS EMAIL had come through from her agent, Richard, that morning, but Celeste had been buried deep in the research for her next chapter, so had put it off until she was ready for her scheduled mid-morning break. Now, as the final credits on the *Christmas Cracker Cranium Quiz* rolled, she smiled to herself.

That hadn't actually been nearly as bad as she'd expected. She'd avoided watching the show when it had aired the night before, partly because she was nervous about how it would turn out, and partly because she'd been having dinner with her parents and some of their department colleagues, and there was no television in the Hunter family home.

She clearly had a friend in the editing suite. Celeste remembered the actual filming as being more confrontational on her side—the way she always got when she was nervous or feeling intimidated. But in the final cut, Theo came across as far more superior, more patronising, than in real life.

Which, she supposed, wasn't entirely inaccurate, as he hadn't given her *any* points for all the questions she'd answered far more correctly than his bloody answer cards had.

Finishing the last gulp of her cup of tea, Celeste turned to her other breaktime indulgence—checking her social media accounts. While she didn't tend to post much, she kept up with the world outside her office through them—they were sort of her guilty pleasure. She mostly followed other historians, archaeologists, researchers and writers—as well as a few university and academic accounts, plus the odd political or news website or reporter. She'd actually had to turn off the notifications on her phone and computer, to stop herself getting distracted when she was working. And she *never* let herself check them first thing in the morning. That was a slippery slope she didn't want to fall down.

Which was why she had no idea she'd become an overnight Internet sensation until she checked her phone.

She blinked at the number of notifications

showing, and tapped through to them, scrolling slowly as she took in the words.

Celeste Hunter doesn't need Theo-bloody-Montgomery mansplaining history to her.

There were screenshots, too. Oh, God, she'd become a meme.

Celeste: I have a PhD in this.

Theo: I have an answer card written by an inadequate researcher. So I must be right!

Celeste: I'm an actual professor of history.

Theo: Yeah, but I have generations of white male privilege on my side. Who do you think they're going to listen to?

There were more. So many more.

Then she remembered the second part of her agent's email. *Call me.*

'So are we thinking the show went well?' she asked, weakly, when Richard picked up.

'For us? Very well.' She could practically hear his grin down the phone line. 'For Theo Montgomery, not so much. Not that that's our problem.'

'I feel kind of bad about that,' Celeste admitted. 'The way the show was edited… I mean, yes, I *was* right. But he wasn't actually so patronising about it in person.'

'Nobody cares what *really* happened, Celeste. You know that.'

'Yeah.' She'd learned, a little, over the past year. After the first radio slot she'd done, as a favour for a friend who'd had to drop out at the last minute, it seemed as if she'd got her name on some sort of list. Suddenly she was every producer's pet historian, trotted out to offer an historical perspective on current events, on school history exams, on latest discoveries and research. No matter that her official area of expertise was ancient history, she'd become a knowledgeable semi-pro on the whole span of human existence. At least it was the one thing her childhood had prepared her for.

And it had led to the talks about her own TV show, looking at women through history— starting with Ancient Greece.

She supposed something like this could only be good publicity, and production companies definitely loved good publicity. No wonder Richard was sounding so thrilled.

'So, we need to capitalise on this,' he went on. 'We need to show that production company that your series is a sure bet. We could have it commissioned by January! Get you on display a bit more, now you've stepped out from behind the radio mic and people know what you look like.'

Celeste pulled a face at that last bit, glad that Richard couldn't see it. On display wasn't exactly her favourite place to be, she'd learned. Especially when it wasn't on her terms.

'What's your calendar like between now and the new year?' Richard asked.

She looked at the stack of research materials, liberally spotted with sticky notes, that were supposed to form the basis of her book. Not even the popular history book she was supposed to be writing to support the case for the TV show, but the *other* one. The proper, serious, academic text that would cement her career at the university—the one her parents would approve of.

The one that was going nowhere at all.

'I have some time,' she told Richard. 'Term ended yesterday, so I don't have any more lectures or seminars to give until January.'

'Great! I'll see if I can get some appearances set up for you, then. Keep in touch!'

And he was gone. Celeste sighed, and put down her phone—until she noticed the new message notification, the one notification she allowed herself, since hardly anyone ever messaged her, was flashing.

Fancy lunch? My treat. Seems like I owe you. Theo Montgomery.

Cerys had been right. He *hated* this idea.

He especially hated the part where he was sitting in a restaurant, alone, with people staring at him, whispering behind his back. He didn't need to be able to make out the individual words to guess what they were saying. Exactly the same things as everyone on social media—and the morning TV shows, apparently—had been saying since the *Christmas Cracker Cranium Quiz* aired. Plus, all the older gossip about Tania and the break-up, probably, just for good measure.

He'd watched the show. He'd read the comments. He'd watched the show *again*.

Then Cerys had called back, given him Celeste's phone number, and told him exactly what he needed to do.

'Make it right, Theo. And quickly.'

He hadn't honestly been sure that Celeste would respond when he texted her. He should have called, probably—Cerys had told him to—but Theo remembered what had happened last time he'd interrupted Celeste, in the green room, and decided that it might go better if he allowed her to respond in her own time, rather than ambushing her with a phone call.

Perhaps it was the right move, because she *had* texted back. And she'd agreed to meet him, here, in a neutral restaurant, ten minutes ago. He checked his watch; no, fifteen now.

Celeste didn't seem like a habitually late person to Theo, but, apparently, he was wrong. That happened a lot. Just ask his parents. *They* still hadn't forgiven him for 'losing' Tania—a rich, beautiful, famous prospective daughter-in-law they would have embraced willingly, despite her 'unfortunate start' on reality TV. His parents always claimed to have incredibly high standards for their social circle, but as far as Theo could tell they mostly all came down to 'money' and 'fame'.

God, what if this debacle lost him both of those? Infamy, he knew, was not the same thing.

Maybe his father would take some comfort in the fact that he'd been right all along, and Theo really would never amount to anything worthwhile. If Celeste didn't show up for this lunch, it might be the best he was going to get.

Finally, after another five minutes, the restaurant door flew open and Celeste Hunter strode in, wrapped in an elegant white wool coat, black boots clicking on the tiled floor as she crossed towards him. Her dark hair was twisted up on the back of her head, her lips painted a bright Christmas red, and she seemed completely unaware of the way every person in the restaurant turned to look at her as she approached him.

Theo was not unaware. He could hear the whispering, the *'Isn't that her?'* that hung in the air behind her.

'I'm sorry I'm late,' she said, stripping off her coat and hanging it on the back of one of the empty chairs. Underneath it, her black jumper matched her black jeans. Her lipstick, Theo realised, was the only colour about her. 'There were all these...people waiting outside my office at the university. Apparently last night's show was a bit of a thing.'

A bit of a thing? Did she really just describe my career-crippling disaster as 'a bit of a thing'?

She had. Because, of course, that was all it was—to her. *Her* career was the university, her academic life. TV was merely a bit on the side.

Whereas it was all he had.

'Apparently so,' he said drily, although she didn't seem to pick up on the faint hint of sarcasm in his voice. 'In fact, some of the rumours online are starting to get a little outlandish. And nasty.'

She had the good grace to wince at that, at

least. 'If only you'd just admitted I was right at the time, huh?'

Theo honestly couldn't tell if she was joking or not. Why was this woman so hard to read? He was *good* at people, usually—it was what had got him as far as he'd come. But this woman? He had no idea what was going on inside her head—or how she was going to react when he put Cerys's plan to her.

She might go along with it. Or she might verbally eviscerate him while pouring hot oil onto his chest on the restaurant table while the crowd cheered her on. It was hard to tell.

He was just going to have to take his chances. But he could at least improve them by softening her up first.

'Thank you for coming, despite everything.' He flashed her his best 'love me' smile, and she looked a little taken aback. Fortunately, the waiter arrived at that moment with the wine he'd ordered, and poured them both a glass.

God, he hoped she liked Viognier, or this would be off to a worse start than ever.

He held his breath as she took a sip, then started to let it out when she smiled at the waiter, only to have it catch in his chest again.

That smile, he thought, as he half choked on his own breath.

She hadn't smiled like that when they were

recording the show. And she definitely hadn't smiled at him like that ever—not even when he'd done nothing beyond politely introduce himself. Yet the waiter got that smile—all bone-deep pleasure and gratitude.

He supposed it was reassuring to know that she *could* smile like that. It might make the next phase of Cerys's plan easier.

Theo took a sip of the wine to soothe his throat after the coughing fit Celeste had totally ignored. It was nice enough wine. But not worthy of that smile.

'This is delicious, thank you,' Celeste said to the waiter. 'Did you suggest it?'

The waiter—young, spotty and obviously impressionable—blushed. 'Um, actually your, uh, companion chose it.'

The smile disappeared as she turned back to Theo. 'Oh, well. It's still nice wine.'

Theo decided to let that one pass while they ordered—Celeste asking the poor waiter what most people ordered, then going with that.

'So.' Celeste folded her hands on her lap, over the napkin the anxious waiter had placed there, and looked Theo dead in the eye. 'I imagine you invited me here to apologise?'

He had, of course. That was step one of Cerys's master plan. But being asked to do so outright like that…it made him want to, well, not.

Theo lifted an eyebrow. 'You don't think there's any reason you should need to apologise to me?'

That earned him a flash of a grin. Nothing like the smile she'd given the waiter for the wine, but still. Better than anything he'd managed from her so far.

'Of course,' she said, her tone heavy with sarcasm. 'I'm so sorry that your mansplaining and patronising behaviour got you into trouble with your adoring fans.'

Theo rolled his eyes. 'Come on, I was actually there too, remember? I haven't just watched the edited footage. I know what really happened.'

She raised both eyebrows, and sat back in her chair. 'Enlighten me, then.'

He wanted to. He wanted to fight his corner, wanted to stand up for what he felt had really happened. But he also wanted all the other people sitting in the restaurant to stop listening to their conversation.

This was never going to work. Cerys hadn't met Celeste, or she'd never have imagined for a moment that it *could* work.

But what other option did he have?

Theo took a deep breath, and started again.

'You're right. I *did* ask you here to apologise. Let's start over, shall we?'

One step at a time, that was all he had to

focus on. If this went well, he might not need all the other steps of Cerys's absurd plan.

He just had to keep the conversation civil for one lunch.

How hard could that be?

Why on earth had she agreed to this lunch? Curiosity, Celeste supposed. The curse of the academic. She just couldn't help but want to know what happened next, and why.

Plus Richard had been pretty insistent, when she'd called him back to ask what to do. Apparently, being seen with Theo Montgomery again, even if she wasn't sure why he wanted to see her at all, was a Good Thing, publicity-wise.

'Keep them talking,' as Richard put it. *'Doesn't matter what they're saying, as long as they're talking about you.'*

But Celeste was pretty sure Theo *did* care what people were saying. Was it just that he was so used to being the Nice Guy he couldn't handle people thinking otherwise? Or was he concerned about the effect on his career?

Or—and this seemed the least likely—was he genuinely sorry about how things had gone down at the filming?

That last went out of the window as he asked if perhaps she should be apologising to *him*, of all things. But then he pulled himself together and she saw something she hadn't expected to see from Theo Montgomery.

Authenticity.

He immediately hid it again, behind that charming smile and smooth words, suggesting they start over. But for a second there, Celeste almost believed she saw the real human behind the TV persona.

And he looked just as baffled and annoyed about this lunch as she was.

Interesting.

She'd pegged him as a faker straight off— she'd had enough students who tried to pretend they'd done the work to know how to spot a faker at a hundred paces. Besides, wasn't that the whole point of TV? To show a faked-up version of reality? Even her own appearance on the quiz show hadn't been authentic—she'd never be caught dead in a Christmas jumper outside that studio.

Some people, she knew, had been faking so long they'd forgotten how to be real. She'd assumed Theo would be one of them.

Apparently, there was still some hope for him after all.

'I'm sorry that the research on our show wasn't up to your own standards,' Theo said, which she noticed wasn't actually a real apology on his own behalf. 'I could tell that you'd prepared well for the show, and to a level that our researchers clearly weren't expecting.' A flash of that charming smile. 'And I'm sorry that I couldn't accept your—obviously correct—answers. I hope you didn't feel that I was mansplaining to you. On the contrary, I had the producer in my ear telling me to read out the official answer—but *I* was far more interested in the answers you were giving.'

Did she believe him? Celeste wasn't sure. But then he went on, 'Is it really true that Prince Albert wasn't responsible for bringing Christmas trees to Britain?'

So, he'd been paying attention. Or he'd just watched the show again in preparation for this lunch.

'Are you questioning me now?'

He held up his hands in surrender. 'I swear to you I'm not. Is it so hard to believe that I might be interested in the answer?'

Yes. Not just because he hadn't been the other night—she could understand that, under the constraints of filming and with his producer talking in his ear, hurrying him along, he might not have had the time or mental space to care about the real answer then. But in her experience, even when she stripped away those problems, most people weren't all that interested in the real answers anyway.

The simple, familiar stories were more interesting. Prince Albert had brought the Christmas tree. Thomas Crapper invented the toilet—except he didn't. Santa Claus was designed by a popular drinks company in the thirties—also not true.

People didn't want the complicated, multi-layered truth—the same way that people didn't want to bother with her, and her difficult to understand nature. They wanted the straightforward historical anecdotes that made sense and that people nodded along with—exactly how they wanted Theo Montgomery and his bland smiles, rather than her, on their TVs every night.

Except…the people who'd posted on social media about the show *had* been interested in her answers. They were cross that Theo had cut her off before she'd fully explained them.

They hadn't said she was boring, unlike most other people outside her family. They'd been *interested*. In her. And maybe it was because it was Christmas, and lots of people were interested in Christmas, right? But if she could get them interested in that—if she could get *Theo freaking Montgomery* interested in that—maybe she could get people interested in the lives of women in the ancient world, too. Maybe she really could pull off her own show.

It had to be worth a try, right?

'Queen Charlotte, the wife of George III, put up the first one in 1800,' she said, watching to see if his eyes glazed over. They didn't. 'Where she grew up, in the duchy of Mecklenburg-Strelitz, Germany, the tradition was to decorate a single yew branch. She brought the tradition over with her in 1761, and the whole palace started getting involved in it. Then in 1800 she was planning a children's party at Windsor and decided to pot up a whole yew tree and decorate it with sweets and baubles and load it with presents. The kids were enchanted, of course, and Christmas trees became all the rage in English high society.'

Theo smiled, looking genuinely charmed at the information. 'I did not know that. Thank you.'

'You're welcome,' she replied, suddenly awkwardly aware that she was basically lecturing her lunch date on British history.

Well, it wasn't as if she had much else in the way of small talk, was it? That was always the problem with her dates, or interactions with people outside the history department. She bored them quickly. Hell, sometimes she even bored herself. She wished that she could just let things go, not feel she had to correct people all the time. But it was as if there were an itch inside her, whenever things were factually lacking. And the only way to scratch it was to present the true facts.

No wonder it had been so long since she'd had an actual date.

The rest of the meal passed pleasantly enough. The waiter brought their meals, which were fine, although Theo questioned her choice of the chicken Caesar salad in the depths of winter.

She shrugged. 'The waiter said it was their most popular dish.' She always ordered the most popular dish. She knew nothing about food, really, and, beyond it being the fuel her body needed to keep functioning, she'd never really thought about it much. So it seemed much more sensible to her to let the consensus of others decide what she should eat.

Theo obviously didn't agree. 'What if the most popular dish was something you didn't like?'

'Then I'd order the second most popular dish. Obviously.'

It was only by the time they'd reached dessert— which she'd declined in favour of coffee, as had Theo—that she got the feeling that there was more to this meal than just a simple apology.

'I have to admit, I had a secondary reason for inviting you to lunch today,' Theo said, as he toyed with the foil wrapper of the mint that came with his coffee.

Wow. Her intuition was actually correct, for once. Delayed, of course, but right. That didn't happen often. At least, not with people she didn't know. Damon and Rachel she could read in an instant—she'd been studying them both for years. She'd *learned* them, the same way she learned everything else. Strangers, not so much.

'I suspected as much,' she said.

Theo smiled. 'I imagined you would. You're an intelligent woman.'

She liked the way he said that. She shouldn't, because she was sure he was just buttering her up for the next part. But when Theo said, 'You're an intelligent woman,' she didn't hear it as an insult. He wasn't saying: 'You have brains, why can't you understand people?' Or: 'You're smart, but don't think you're smarter than me.' Or even: 'You're intelligent, why won't you just agree with me, when I'm obviously right?'

He was just saying that she was intelligent, and that it was a good thing.

She liked that.

'So? Why am I here?' Celeste asked.

Theo drew in a breath, then looked up and met her gaze with his own. She made herself hold it, look for the truth, even though she wanted to look away with every fibre of her being. She didn't look people in the eye like this, not unless she had a point she needed to hammer home and wanted to be sure they had it.

But now she was just…listening. And looking for the truth in Theo's eyes.

'Because the show that aired last night was edited to show me in a bad light. I don't know why, or by who. And I need you to believe that I didn't intend to dismiss you or disregard the points you were making about historical accuracy.'

'Why?' That was the part she didn't understand. Why did he care what *she* thought?

'Because I'm going to need your help to fix it.'

CHAPTER FOUR

CELESTE DREW BACK a little at that. 'What do you need me to do?'

'Exactly what you are doing,' Theo replied, as reassuringly as he could. 'Just being seen with me today, showing that you don't actually hate me, that will help.'

She looked around her. 'You mean, you've got someone here to photograph us together? This was all a trick to get me to pretend to like you?'

Ow. 'I was kind of hoping that if we had lunch together you would *actually* like me. Most people do, you know.'

'I'm not most people.' As if he didn't know that. 'So, where is he? The photographer, I mean? I haven't seen anyone taking photos of us. Does he have one of those long lenses?'

'I didn't hire a paparazzi with a tele-focus lens,' Theo said patiently. 'I didn't hire anybody. I didn't need to.'

Celeste's eyes narrowed. 'Explain.'

'Celeste, people have been taking photos of us on their phones since the moment you walked in. They've been talking about us, while we've been sitting here eating. There's hardly a table in this restaurant where at least one person hasn't turned to watch us, to try to listen to what we're saying.' He was used to it, after years in the TV spotlight. Normally when he dined with someone from outside the industry they found it distracting, disturbing to be watched all the time.

But Celeste hadn't noticed it at all.

'Why? Because you're so damn famous and popular?' She was glancing around now, furtively, obviously trying to catch someone with their phone out. It was kind of almost cute—if anything about Celeste Hunter could be called cute.

And she obviously didn't realise how unpopular he was right now. He supposed she didn't really follow celebrity gossip online.

'Because our faces were all over their social media feeds this morning,' he said, with a sigh. 'Because if other people are talking about us, they want to be able to talk about us, too. And if they can say something new, something their friends haven't heard yet, all the better.'

'So this morning the story was that we were mortal enemies after a stupid quiz show,' Celeste said slowly. 'And you're trying to change that narrative. Show people that actually we're friends.'

'Exactly.' He'd known she'd get it, once she got past the part where people she'd never met cared about her life. As he'd said, she was an intelligent woman.

'I probably shouldn't tip my cup of coffee into your lap for manipulating me into lunch, then, should I?' she asked sweetly.

Theo winced. 'Ideally not, no. And I didn't intend to manipulate you. I kind of thought it would be obvious.'

'Yeah, well. You might have noticed I'm not entirely up to speed on things that happen outside my field of expertise.'

It was the first admission of anything approaching a fault or weakness that she'd given, and it made Theo like her all the more.

That was the strangest part about this lunch, he realised. He was actually enjoying it. Even when they were bickering or she was threatening his lap with coffee, he was having *fun*.

Huh. He really hadn't expected that.

'So, what do you say?' he asked. 'Do you want to pretend to be my friend and help rehabilitate my reputation, so the Great British Public can stop calling me a patronising, mansplaining bastard?' Amongst all the things they'd already been saying about him before, about him being a careless, unfeeling abandoner of women.

She looked at him thoughtfully. 'You realise there's also a cohort of your defenders calling me an uppity bitch who thinks she knows better than everyone?'

'Yeah, but you *do* know better than everyone—when it comes to history anyway.'

'Not everyone. Just most people.'

'And you're not an uppity bitch. In fact, I think I might actually like you if you'll let me get to know you.' She looked surprised at that, and he laughed. 'Yeah. I wasn't expecting that, either.'

Although he *had* been—until he'd met her. When she was just a voice on the radio, he'd thought he would like to get to know her. He'd been drawn to the passion in her voice when she'd talked about subjects she cared about— that he cared about, too. So yeah, he'd wanted to get to know her. He just hadn't expected it to be under these circumstances.

'Maybe we can prove them all wrong, then,' she said slowly. 'Or at least teach them not to judge people or their motives on first appearances.'

Theo rather thought she was crediting them with too much power over social media in general, and the Great British Public in particular. But if that was what it took to get her to agree…

'I say we could give it a damn good go.'

Celeste looked up at him and smiled. 'Then it's a deal.'

She stood up, holding out a hand for him to shake, and the movement jogged the table. The tablecloth caught between her and the surface, twisting as she moved, tugging it up, off balance and…

Tipping Theo's coffee right into his lap.

A gasp went up through the restaurant, and Theo heard the click of a dozen fake camera shutters on phones.

He looked up to find Celeste with one hand over her mouth, looking as though she was trying to stop herself from laughing.

'At least it wasn't *my* coffee,' she said as she handed him her napkin.

'That makes it all better,' Theo grumbled.

Apparently, making people believe they were actually friends was going to be even harder than he'd anticipated.

It looked like Theo and Celeste were a story that wasn't going away.

On Sunday morning, Celeste woke up to a lot of social media notifications, and a sense of impending doom. The doom part was easy enough to fathom—it was the first Sunday of the month, which meant it was Hunter family dinner day. Which was cause enough for doomy feelings in itself, but made worse by the fact that she wasn't properly prepared for it.

It wasn't enough for her parents to get the four of them around the dining table once a month for a nice catch-up and a roast. Diana and Jacob Hunter had to make it a competition. One with themes and decorations and complex menus— and one that Celeste always tried hard at but seldom ever won.

She definitely wasn't going to win anything today, having spent all her prep time yesterday either having lunch with Theo or on the phone with Rachel, who'd sounded very peculiar when she'd called. Celeste might not be the best at reading people normally, but *Rachel* she understood. They'd been best friends since university and she was, as Damon put it, Celeste's social proof that she could actually manage human interaction outside the lecture theatre.

She had a strong suspicion that her brother might be behind her best friend's strange mood. Damon, unlike her, was excellent with people— all people. Often too excellent. Women, in particular, tended to fall fast and hard for him—only to be heartbroken when he let them down, however gently he tried to do it.

Rachel had known Damon for almost a decade, so Celeste had hoped she was immune. But after her disappearance from the TV studios, plus that call last night... Celeste was starting to have suspicions.

Which were definitely still on her mind as she went shopping for ingredients for an emergency starter she could whip up in a hurry in time for lunch. Salmon, perhaps. Damon hated salmon.

Queueing at the supermarket checkout, she scrolled through the notifications on her phone. Gone were the usual links to journals or news items about archaeological digs she had come to expect. Instead, there were at least four different photo angles of Theo getting covered in coffee, plus a few other shots of them just eating lunch together. Opinion seemed to be divided over whether they were arguing or having a nice time.

Both. Which she supposed was why people were so confused. It was baffling the hell out of her.

Normally, when she argued with a person, they got annoyed and left her alone. But Theo seemed to want to spend *more* time together. Which was definitely not normal.

It's only because he's trying to save face, improve his image, that sort of thing.

She needed to keep reminding herself of that. He was a faker, and he'd fake liking her for as long as it served his purpose—then drop her. In some ways, Theo was like Damon—too charming for his own good. Luckily Celeste, unlike Rachel, *was* immune to that sort of charm.

And it wasn't only Theo's career and image that stood to gain from this association, it turned out. Richard was thrilled that their continued association was only drawing more attention to her—and increasing the odds of the production company they were talking to taking a chance on her. As a cloistered academic, she knew he'd been at a bit of a loss on how to market her—especially since her love of *reading* social media didn't extend to remembering to post regularly, or even having any idea what to post. Rachel kept offering her tips. Maybe she should just hire her best friend to pretend to be her on social media. She had no doubt that people would like her better if she wasn't, well, actually her.

'Excuse me. Are you... Oh, what's your name? The one from that quiz show. The Christmas Cracker one.' The woman behind her in the queue, gripping a TV listing magazine with Theo Montgomery on the front, smiled up at Celeste.

'The *Christmas Cracker Cranium Quiz*? Yes, that was me.' Celeste waited to see if that was a good thing or a bad thing.

The woman's beaming smile grew wider. 'I thought it was you! I said to my husband—where's he gone? Fred? Honestly, men. Anyway, I said it was you!'

'And it is, actually, me,' Celeste confirmed, just in case that had got missed somehow.

'Can you sign my magazine for me?' The woman brandished a pen towards Celeste, and she took it, mostly because she was at a loss as to what else to do with it. As she signed her name just to the left of Theo's sharp cheekbone, the woman kept talking. 'I love Theo Montgomery as much as anybody, and I never really believed all that rubbish his ex put about, but, I have to say, it was quite nice to see him put in his place for once! He always has all the answers, doesn't he? Such a charmer. My Fred says he's *too* smooth, but, really, what would we watch if he wasn't on? He hosts all the best shows these days, doesn't he?'

'I suppose he does.' Celeste handed the signed magazine back.

'And he *is* lovely, don't you think?' the woman said wistfully.

'I'm sure I wouldn't know.' Celeste turned away, relieved to see it was her turn at the checkout at last.

All this thinking about Theo Montgomery couldn't possibly be good for her.

* * *

She managed to forget about him, more or less, over lunch with the family.

The Hunter Family Monthly Lunch was, as most things were in her family, deeply competitive. Each month, she, her mother and her father were assigned a course of the meal to prepare and serve. Whoever was in charge of starters was also in charge of decorating the dining room in a suitable historical theme. Damon was only ever in charge of bringing the wine, because he refused to compete.

The aim of the dinner was to produce the most interesting dish. Not necessarily the most delicious—Celeste had once won almost a full score from everyone for an authentic Greek dish with a great historical backstory that had unfortunately tasted like rotten fish. Mostly because it almost *was* rotten fish.

On that basis, she knew she'd have failed today. The only saving grace her salmon terrine possessed was that it would annoy her brother, and her decorations were decidedly sub-par.

And sadly, none of that distracted her mother from more important matters at hand.

'I saw some of that festive TV show you were associated with, Celeste,' Diana said, her frown disapproving over the fluttering of her authentic replica regency fan, to match her dress. The

Hunters always believed in dressing for dinner, even if they weren't always from the same era.

'Uh...really? Where did you see that?' Stalling for time, Celeste reached across the table for the wine bottle and refilled her mother's glass, as well as her own. At least her father was out of the room, fetching his main course from the kitchen. She'd hoped against hope that her parents' TV ban would mean they'd have missed the whole debacle, but apparently she wasn't that lucky.

'A colleague sent me a web link to a clip from it.' Diana's fan fluttered a little faster. Across the table, a wicked smile spread over Damon's face.

Celeste knew exactly what he was thinking. Discovering that Celeste was taking part in a lowbrow, populist TV quiz was one thing. Being told so by a colleague was far worse, because that meant that Other People knew. People that mattered to their parents.

She wondered who had sent it to them. Someone who thought it was a bit of festive fun? Or a colleague with a grudge? It didn't really matter which, she supposed. The Professors Hunter didn't *do* fun—at least, not when it came to things that mattered, like history or archaeology, their respective specialist subjects.

'Um, which part?' Celeste asked, desperately

hoping that the clip would be one of the tamer ones she'd seen around the Internet. Maybe the introductions, or something.

'You, arguing with some gameshow host about how Christmas trees came to be a British tradition.'

So, not a nice tame bit. That was the part that had the Internet most riled up. Of course.

Damon was apparently unable to hold his laughter in a moment longer.

'That link is everywhere, Mum,' he said as Celeste glared at him. 'Have you seen what they're saying about it on Twitter?' He leaned across the table towards Celeste. 'Did you *really* have a make-up lunch with Theo yesterday? The whole of social media is aflame, wondering what's going on between you two.'

Celeste felt the heat flood to her cheeks as she remembered the lunch—and how it had ended. Then she remembered why she was cross with Damon in the first place, and turned the tables.

'Never mind my lunch. Did you *really* take Rachel for afternoon tea at the Ritz?'

'It was for work!' Damon protested, far too quickly for Celeste's liking. 'She's helping out on my latest project.'

'Isn't Rachel an English graduate?' Diana asked. 'How is she going to help with your... what was it? Cinema project?'

'The cinema project was two years ago,' Damon said. 'This is a new one.'

Of course, it was. It was always a new project with Damon. Always the next shiny thing.

Celeste didn't want him treating Rachel that way. And while she was pretty sure he wouldn't, pretty sure wasn't enough when it came to her best friend. 'Just…be careful with Rachel, please? I'd hate for you to, well, give her any ideas.'

'It's work,' he repeated, his voice flat. 'That's all.'

Work was good. Rachel had been stuck in her job, working for her stepmother, for too long. Doing something new and fun with Damon could be good for her. As long as it really was just work.

Rachel didn't date much, and, after a nasty experience with one of her stepsisters' friends the summer before, Celeste couldn't see her jumping into anything new. But it *was* Damon. And Rachel had always been just a little bit misty-eyed when it came to Celeste's brother.

She had to warn him about that. He'd be careful if he thought he might hurt her. He wasn't a bad guy, just…not the settling-down type. With anything.

'Good,' Celeste said, looking away as she spilled her best friend's secrets for her own good. 'Because, to be honest, I think she's always had a bit of a crush on you. I'd hate for you to lead her on, even accidentally.' Urgh, she hated doing this. 'Just don't break her heart, okay? I know what you're like.'

The double doors to the dining room swung open and their father appeared, the white of his Roman-style toga backlit by the hallway bulbs against the dim candlelight on the table. In his arms was a large platter with what looked like an entire pig on it, apple in mouth and all, surrounded by jellies with apple slices and spices inside.

'Dinner is served!' Jacob announced, holding the platter high, a smug smile on his face.

Celeste laughed, and turned her attention back to lunch, happy to forget all about Damon's love life—and her own fake one—for the afternoon.

Having hot coffee dumped in his lap wasn't, in Theo's opinion, the best way to spend a date. But by Monday morning, his lunch with Celeste seemed to be having the desired effect, at least.

'She's good for you,' Cerys announced, when she'd finished cackling at the photo of Celeste trying to hide her own laughter as he mopped up the coffee with a napkin, which was doing the rounds on social media that morning. 'If you can convince people she actually likes you—or, even better, wants you—it'll help give the impression that there's more to you than just a pretty face.'

Theo didn't ask if *Cerys* believed that there was more to him than his looks. He wasn't sure he wanted to hear the answer.

But the ultimate confirmation came as he walked into a meeting late on Monday morning with all the bigwigs involved in the *New Year's Eve Spectacular* he'd hopefully still be hosting in just a few weeks.

It might have been hard to think about the new year with Christmas still around the corner, but after the debacle of the *Christmas Cracker Cranium Quiz* Theo was more than happy to just skip the festive period altogether and start fresh on January the first.

'Good to see you keeping your face in the spotlight ahead of the big show,' one of them told Theo as he took his seat.

'I heard it wasn't his face, so much,' another murmured, loud enough to be heard around the table. Theo ignored them and reached for the coffee pot. 'Careful with that, old boy. Heard coffee's a bit of a sensitive issue for you right now.'

That caused a wave of laughter that cascaded through the room. It irritated him, but Theo had learned many years ago not to let that show. His father loved to see the effect of his jibes and would keep needling if he thought he was close to getting a reaction. Making Theo blow up had been easy when he was a boy, harder as he became a teenager and learned not to play the game.

These days, one of his bestselling points was his easy-going nature, his ability to take a joke at his own expense and keep smiling. Something to thank his father for, he supposed.

Always smiling. That was the job.

'Well, at least I got lunch with a beautiful woman first,' he joked, pouring his coffee without spilling a drop.

That, of course, just opened up a new flood of questions.

'What really is going on with you two?' Matthew, from Finance, asked. 'I read online that you've been secretly dating for months. And Fran said it was you who suggested getting Celeste on the show, so…' He left it hanging, an open question.

Theo considered how best to answer, Cerys's words still echoing around his head.

If you can convince people she actually likes you—or, even better, wants you—it'll help give the impression that there's more to you than just a pretty face.

Wasn't that what he wanted people to believe? He'd asked Celeste to help him rehabilitate his reputation—but now he wondered if she could do more. Could being seen with her help him persuade his bosses, and maybe even the Great British Public, that there was more to him than just the ability to smile on cue?

Maybe that was asking too much. But it could be a start...

'You know me, Matthew,' he replied, with that smile he was so famous for. 'I don't kiss and tell. Now, what's on the agenda for today?'

There was still plenty to discuss before the filming date, so he managed to keep the group around the table more or less on topic for the rest of the meeting. But as they all filed out, Mr Erland, one of the real bigwigs, held Theo back.

'I just wanted to say—I was worried, after Friday night. I thought we might have to look at replacing you for New Year, if the country was against you. But you seem to be turning it around.'

Theo's heart thumped in his chest. 'I'm certainly trying, sir.'

Mr Erland slapped him on the back. 'And I always back a trier. Keep it up, Theo, and we'll see you right.'

Hands in his suit pockets, he headed out after

the others, whistling a Christmas carol Theo remembered singing in school.

Once he was sure he was gone, he reached for his phone, and scrolled through for the latest name added to its memory.

Celeste answered promptly, but, from the click-clacking he could hear in the background, she didn't stop typing while she spoke to him.

'Yes?' No messing around with unnecessary words for Celeste. It was kind of refreshing, after a meeting that had seemed to be seventy per cent waffle.

'Are you free this afternoon? Well, this evening, really, I suppose.' It was already almost two, and he needed to eat lunch and deal with some emails before anything else.

'Which is it, Theo? Afternoon or evening?' The typing sounds paused for a second, while she waited for his answer. Theo smiled.

'Is your answer different depending on which one I pick?' Dropping into one of the abandoned chairs, he kicked his feet up onto the meeting table and leaned back on two chair legs.

'No. I just like a little precision in my scheduling.' Of course, she did.

'Four-thirty, then. At Hyde Park.' He grinned as the plan came together in his head. 'I want to show you a Winter Wonderland.'

'You mean *the* Winter Wonderland, I assume?' she corrected him. 'Fairground rides and stalls and such? For kids?'

'Not just kids,' Theo countered. 'It's actually one of my favourite things about London at Christmas.'

'Of course, it is.' She sighed. 'Fine, I'll meet you there at four-thirty. Which gate?'

Theo considered, mentally reviewing the map of the place in his head. He'd been there often enough to know the basic layout. 'The Green Gate,' he decided. It was closest to the Bavarian village, and he had a feeling he'd need a glühwein by then. 'I'll see you there.'

He was about to hang up, when he realised that Celeste hadn't. He waited and, after a moment, she spoke again.

'So…we're really doing this? Pretending to be friends?'

Theo thought back to what he'd told his colleagues earlier. At some point, he'd have to break it to Celeste that he was hoping they could pretend to be *more* than friends. At that point, he figured he'd either get a glühwein to the face, or maybe, just maybe, a kiss for the cameras that were bound to be hanging around the Hyde Park winter attraction.

He'd much, much rather the kiss, he decided. And not just because he'd had enough drinks thrown over him lately.

'I told you,' he said, after too long a beat. 'Most people end up *actually* liking me, once they get to know me.' Silence from the other end of the line. 'But if you have to pretend, yeah, I'll take that, too.' He knew when to admit defeat.

'Then I'll see you at four-thirty,' Celeste said, and hung up.

CHAPTER FIVE

'MOST PEOPLE END up actually *liking me, once they get to know me.'*

Theo's words were still fresh in Celeste's mind as she hopped off the Tube at Hyde Park Corner, wound her scarf a little tighter around her neck, and headed in the direction of noise, lights and Christmas music.

She hadn't wanted to tell him that actually liking him was exactly what she was afraid of.

Lunch with him had been fun, apart from the coffee incident. And even that had been kind of funny, if she thought about it. Most people she knew would have been furious to find themselves suddenly doused in hot coffee, but Theo had merely rolled his eyes and mopped up the mess. At least it hadn't been boiling, she supposed.

And yes, they'd bickered for most of the lunch, but even *that* had been fun. It turned out she didn't mind people disagreeing with her quite so much when they actually listened to her reasoned arguments and, sometimes at least, changed their mind off the back of them. She was so used to arguing with people who held such deeply entrenched opinions they'd never change them, whatever evidence she presented, that Theo was a lovely change.

He even seemed genuinely interested in her historical knowledge—something she definitely hadn't expected after the *Christmas Cracker Cranium Quiz* debacle.

But none of that meant that she should start liking him, for one, very good reason.

He didn't like her.

He was pretending to, obviously, to convince the Great British Public that he wasn't a mansplaining, patronising, patriarchal idiot. He was a faker. Pretending was what he did. But he didn't actually *like* her. Very few people did. Rachel, possibly Damon. Maybe one or two of her colleagues or students, from time to time. She wasn't honestly sure about her parents. She'd always worked more on winning their respect, professionally, than worrying about whether they *liked* her.

It had never bothered her before. She had the people that mattered to her, and she had her work. Everything else was basically surplus to requirements. She knew she wasn't always easy to get along with, that her priorities weren't always the same as other people's. But she had the respect of the people who mattered, who made decisions about her career and her future.

What else could she want?

Except suddenly, ridiculously, she wanted Theo Montgomery to like her, the way she liked spending time with him. And that was stupid, so she was going to push it aside and focus on the fact that they were *pretending* to like each other for reasons entirely to do with their careers and nothing to do with them as people.

'Easy,' she said, out loud, gaining an odd look from a small girl in a princess costume who was walking along the path towards the Winter Wonderland with her parents.

Celeste ignored that, too.

Hyde Park's Winter Wonderland was quite the spectacle. Celeste had never been before, although she knew groups of colleagues from the university had organised trips in past years. It would be easy to get lost, especially with only the poorly drawn and not-to-scale map she'd printed out before leaving the university to guide her. She was glad that she'd insisted that Theo specify which gate they should meet at, as there were four, all leading to different areas of the fair in which to start their exploration. She was relieved to see that Theo had chosen the one nearest the Bavarian village, rather than the ice-skating rink. She'd never actually been skating, but she was willing to bet she'd fall over a lot. She wasn't clumsy, usually. But she made a point of sticking to what she was good at, rather than risking being bad at something new.

Another reason not to try and be friends with Theo. Making friends was most certainly something she wasn't good at.

She spotted Theo almost instantly, leaning against a lamppost, his expensive-looking wool coat and what had to be a cashmere scarf lit by the soft glow. His face was as ridiculously perfect as on the telly, and for a moment Celeste was thrown back to that moment in the green room when he'd interrupted her work. She'd looked up and seen the most attractive man she'd ever met in real life smiling down at her, and panicked.

So she'd done what she always did, and gone into what Damon called her 'superior professor' mode.

Apparently, it took more than abject rudeness to drive Theo Montgomery away when his career was on the line, though. As she approached, he looked up and smiled as he saw her. Pushing away from the lamppost, he headed straight for her.

'You came!'

'You thought I wouldn't?' Maybe she shouldn't have. Maybe she should have stayed safe in her small office, her small, contained and organised life.

No. She was overthinking this. Hadn't she spent yesterday reminding herself that she was immune to charm, and all that stuff? This was a career decision, pure and simple.

She pasted on a smile, and Theo recoiled.

'What?' She let the smile drop.

'That's better,' he said, looking relieved. 'I was afraid you were going to throw glühwein over me before we even got inside.'

Celeste held up her empty hands. 'No glühwein.'

Grinning, Theo grabbed one hand and held it in his own. 'Well, that will never do. Let's go find you some. You can drink while we explore, and then we can talk.'

'Talk?' Everything was moving so fast. Theo's words, his long stride, the spinning lights of the Ferris wheel in the distance. 'We need to talk?'

'Absolutely. And I'd definitely like to do it once we've both *finished* our drinks this time.'

She couldn't help but laugh at that.

Theo slid her a sideways look as they strolled into the Winter Wonderland. 'That's better.'

'What's better?'

'That smile,' Theo replied. 'That's a real smile—not whatever that terrifying thing at the gate was.'

'Yes, I suppose it was.' A real smile. A real laugh. How long had it been since she'd had those things with anyone who wasn't Rachel or Damon? Too long. Way too long.

Still gripping her hand in his, Theo led her towards the Bavarian village, with its cosy wooden chalets and strings of lights illuminating the crowds.

'Come on,' he said. 'Glühwein waits for no one.'

Maybe this wasn't such a terrible idea, Celeste thought as they approached the nearest stall. Maybe this was just what she needed.

Maybe it was the glühwein, or maybe the intrinsic excitement of the Winter Wonderland experience, but Celeste seemed charmed by the evening. Even Theo's ego wasn't big enough to assume that was due to his company. But she'd laughed at his jokes and hardly complained about the accuracy of the Bavarian-ness of the village—low—at all.

Okay, it had to be the glühwein, because Theo was actually having fun.

'How do you feel about ice skating?' he asked as they passed by the outdoor rink.

'Faintly panicky,' Celeste admitted, a show of weakness he hadn't expected from her.

It seemed the more time they spent together, the more she relaxed and showed him the woman behind the prickly, know-it-all exterior.

'We'll save that for another day, then. Ferris wheel?' She gave him a doubtful look. 'Want to just drink more glühwein and maybe find some roasted chestnuts?' he tried again.

Celeste looked relieved. 'That sounds good.'

'You're not much for doing things outside your comfort zone, are you?' Theo asked, as they found a table outside one of the pseudo-Bavarian chalets to enjoy the glühwein.

'I went on your stupid gameshow, didn't I?' she countered. 'Although who possibly thought that I'd be a good guest, I can't imagine.'

Theo winced. 'That…that might have been me, actually.'

'Oh.' Celeste blinked a few times, her eyes round in the glow of the fairy lights. 'I…wait. How did you even know I existed?'

He shrugged. 'I'd heard you on the radio a few times. You know how it goes, you've never heard of a person before but suddenly, once you've heard them once, they seem to pop up all over the place.' It was all down to the Baader-Meinhof Phenomenon, Theo knew. A frequency illusion, that owed everything to the brain's pre-disposition to patterns and nothing to fate.

See? He knew stuff, too.

'I've only been on the radio half a dozen times,' Celeste said slowly. 'And only on historical or political programmes. I wouldn't have thought they'd be your cup of tea.'

'I'm interested in lots of things,' Theo replied vaguely.

He wasn't about to tell her about the part-time history degree he'd been studying long distance for the last couple of years. His first attempt at university had ended in failure when he'd dropped out in his second year, and lucked into a TV gig through a random acquaintance. He hadn't been prepared to study then, at eighteen and nineteen, and he hadn't been at all interested in his course—it had ultimately been the subject with the least competition to get into his chosen university. Or rather, the university his parents had expected him to attend, all while telling him he wasn't really bright enough to be there. Looking back, *of course* he'd dropped out—and his father would never let him forget it.

Now he was older, well, he had more respect for and interest in learning. It was fascinating to be studying again, something that really held his attention this time. And he *definitely* hadn't told his parents—or anyone else—that he was doing it.

But he knew his tinkering around the edges of academic study was nothing compared to Celeste's career, so he didn't mention it.

She still looked suspicious, though. Time to change the subject.

'What do you think of the Winter Wonderland?' he asked.

Celeste studied their surroundings thoroughly before answering the question, so Theo found himself doing the same. He took in the busyness, the noise, the lights, the music, the kids, the stalls, the rides… He had always loved the chaos of it all, but, seeing it through Celeste's eyes, he found he could only see the things he knew people complained about in reviews.

Still, when he turned back to Celeste, she was smiling. 'I like it,' she said simply, and Theo felt something inside his chest relax. Then she turned that studious, assessing gaze onto him, and he tensed up again. 'Now. You said we needed to talk?'

He had said that, yes. He was regretting it now, though. It was one thing to *imagine* that Celeste might toss another drink over him when he confessed that he'd hinted to his colleagues that they were actually dating. It was another entirely to facilitate it by confessing.

But it was the right thing to do. Well, the right thing was probably not to lie about it in the first place, but since that ship had sailed…

Theo took a long gulp of his glühwein and tried to think about the best way to broach the subject.

Celeste got there first.

'Is this about all the theories about us online?' she asked. 'My brother tells me that his favourite is the one where we've secretly been dating for months, and were having a lovers' tiff the day of the filming. And, I suppose, when we had lunch. Given the coffee incident,' she added thoughtfully.

He watched as she finished off her glühwein. Perfect. He'd buy her another, if she wanted, after this. But first…

'Is it so bad if people think we're dating?' he asked innocently.

Her gaze turned sharp, apparently totally unaffected by the alcohol. 'Who did you tell that we're dating?'

How did she know? 'I didn't *tell* anyone. I just…might not have corrected people when they assumed.'

Celeste tilted her head to the side as she studied him. Theo shifted uncomfortably, feeling like an artefact in a museum that she was trying to puzzle out. The Rosetta Stone, perhaps. Or one of those carvings that made no sense until you looked at them upside down.

'Why?' she asked finally. Apparently, she couldn't read everything about him, after all. That was strangely reassuring. 'I mean, I know you wanted people to think you were a nice guy again and everything, but that doesn't mean you have to let people think you're actually interested in me. It's not like anyone is genuinely going to believe that I'm your type.'

Theo blinked at that. 'Why wouldn't they believe that? I mean, I'm not sure I really have a type. But you're beautiful, intelligent, funny—'

'I am not funny.'

Of course, *that* was the one she objected to. Theo grinned. 'Yes, you are. You might not always mean to be, but I find you hilarious.'

It was just as well her glass was empty, he decided as she gave it a meaningful look.

'The point is,' he went on, reaching over to take her hand—partly for comfort, partly so she couldn't make a grab for his still-half-full glass, 'anyone would believe I'd want to date you.'

'Even after that show?'

'Especially after that. Did you watch it back? You positively sparkled that night. You were fiery and authentic—and you were right.'

'I was wearing a Christmas jumper.'

'That didn't make you any less right. Or less passionate.' He stroked his finger across the back of her hand, absently. As if it was the most natural thing in the world. And she was watching him do it, he realised. Not stopping him, just watching. 'You had confidence in your knowledge, and in yourself. Trust me, that's very sexy.'

Her gaze shot up to meet his at that, and he saw the astonishment in her eyes. He got the impression people didn't call Celeste Hunter sexy very often. Probably through fear. Because whatever else she was, with those long legs and heeled boots, that dark hair pinned back to reveal her bright, smart eyes…she was definitely sexy. Or maybe Theo had some sort of academic fetish. That wasn't impossible.

'You think I'm sexy?' she asked, in disbelief.

'Who wouldn't?' he countered. 'In fact, the much bigger problem is going to be convincing the Great British Public that you're interested in *me*.'

She smiled at that. Then, without looking down, she turned her hand over under his, so their palms touched. 'We're really doing this, then? Pretending to date, just to improve our professional reputations?'

Theo lifted her hand to his lips and kissed it. 'You know, I think we are.'

* * *

Sitting in her office on Tuesday morning, Celeste stared at the photograph on her phone screen. Apparently, they'd been observed together at the Winter Wonderland, and by more than one person if all the different camera angles she'd seen on social media were anything to go by.

She wasn't surprised they'd been photographed, not any more. Theo was a big name in the country, a national boyfriend, almost. People were interested in what he was up to—and, after their fight on TV, together they were a curiosity.

What surprised her was herself. Or rather, her image in the photograph.

She looked happy. Not in an 'all her students turned in their essays on time' way. Not even in a 'knowing exactly how to end this next chapter' or a 'finding the primary source evidence to solidify her case' way. But in an unguarded, relaxed, 'having fun' way.

It was weird.

Oh, she had fun, of course—but only with people she knew well. Which basically meant Rachel, Damon, and a few acquaintances from the university. She'd expect to see herself looking that way at a conference dinner, perhaps, where she was surrounded by people who cared about the same things she did, who were interested in what she had to say because of her reputation, her academic successes.

This wasn't that.

The photo in question showed them sitting outside one of the Bavarian village chalets, drinking glühwein and chatting. But Theo's hand was resting on hers, and he was leaning towards her as if what she had to say were the most interesting thing he'd ever heard.

It's all an act, she reminded herself. He's an actor. A faker.

But she wasn't. And she knew the joy on her face was real.

She liked spending time with Theo, in a way she hadn't enjoyed a new acquaintance's company since…she couldn't remember when. And that could get dangerous.

Celeste shook her head. She'd be careful. Besides, almost everyone in the world started to irritate her after a while; Theo would be no different, she was sure. Right now it was fun, but they didn't actually have anything in common, beyond the fact they both wanted their TV projects to be a success. That was all.

And so, when her phone rang again, and Theo's name flashed across the screen replacing the photo of them together, she took a breath, answered, and said, 'So, what's our next move?'

* * *

Of course, Celeste reflected a few days later, she hadn't expected the next move to include wearing a swimming costume, outside, in mid December.

'Are you sure about this?' she asked, pulling the fluffy bathrobe she'd been given at the entrance tighter around her.

'Absolutely!' Theo's own bathrobe was tossed over his shoulder, as if the cold didn't bother him anyway. His surf shorts couldn't be much warmer than her one-piece, but they did show off his lightly muscled chest and broad shoulders nicely.

Not that she was looking.

Or was she supposed to be looking? If she was really dating him, she'd be looking, right?

She peeked over at him.

Yeah, she'd definitely be looking. There was a reason Theo was such a favourite on Saturday night TV, and it wasn't all to do with his smile.

He wasn't looking at her, though. He was striding ahead, along the deck of the boat he'd brought her to. It was more of a floating platform, really, Celeste decided. With a bar in the middle, some high cocktail tables, a sturdy rail around the outside, and, of course, the hot tubs at either end.

Celeste followed Theo as he stopped and

spoke to people he passed, even posing for a selfie with a group on girls on a hen night. Then, as he reached the far end, he turned back to take her hand, his gaze not leaving her face for a moment.

Good. That was good. She didn't want him ogling her anyway, even if she was mostly covered by her bathrobe.

Although it probably meant she should stop ogling him. Damn.

'Ready?' Theo asked.

'As I'll ever be.' She paused by the edge of the hot tub.

'You realise you have to take the robe off, right?'

'Unfortunately.'

It wasn't that Celeste was insecure about her body. It was just that it wasn't something she often flaunted like this. Usually she was safely tucked up in her personal uniform of black jeans and boots, with a black top. She went a little different with her winter coat—that was white. But otherwise, her only colour tended to come from her bright lipstick. She wanted people looking at her lips and the words she was saying, after all, not her clothes. Plus, it made getting dressed in the morning a whole lot simpler when she didn't have to worry about things going together.

She swallowed. It wasn't as if anyone would

be looking at her anyway. And her swimming costume was basically an extension of her normal wardrobe—boring and black. Nobody would even notice it next to the highly coloured and patterned bikinis on show.

Celeste let the robe fall from her shoulders and turned to place it over one of the loungers beside the hot tub. When she turned back, Theo's gaze remained focussed firmly on her face, although she couldn't help but notice that his jaw was clenched. Was that with the effort of not looking at her swimsuit-clad body?

God, I hope so. The thought caught her by surprise, and she slipped into the water quickly to try and wash it away.

She didn't want Theo looking at her that way—unless it was to make her feel less bad about looking at *him* that way.

'So, what on earth made you think that an outdoor hot tub on the Thames in December was a good idea for our next "date"?' she asked as Theo handed her a glass of champagne.

Settling into the ledge seat around the edge of the hot tub, Celeste let the bubbles pop against her body, the warmth of the water welcome after the chilly winter air, and took a sip of the champagne, letting *those* bubbles pop against her tongue. Somehow, her shoulders already seemed less tense, as if the stress of hunching over her computer all day getting nowhere were seeping out of her into the water.

'That.' Theo sounded smug as he spoke. 'That's what gave me the idea. Wanting to put that look on your face.'

'What look?' Celeste scowled, but it only made him laugh.

'Not that one. The one you had before, when you took your first sip of champagne. You looked like the worries of the world were lifting from your shoulders.' He smirked at her. 'You're too tense, Celeste. I knew that the first moment you snapped at me in the green room.'

'You interrupted me while I was working,' she pointed out. 'So what, now it's your mission to destress me?'

'Perhaps.' Something changed in his smile. She couldn't figure out what exactly, since she wasn't even sure that his lips had moved at all. But suddenly it felt more secret, more private— and warmer, somehow. Maybe it was his eyes, or the lighting on the boat. That was it, just the lighting. Nothing to do with him, or her, at all.

Faker, she reminded herself, silently. *He's a faker.*

She looked away—and in doing so, noticed that they were being watched.

It was hard to whisper to Theo without getting closer; making herself heard over the bub-

bles was a challenge, and doing so without
the guy sitting on her other side hearing even
harder. So she shifted a little under the water
until she could feel Theo's thigh pressed up
against her own.

Glancing up, she saw him swallow, and his
gaze flashed down, just for a moment, in the direction of her cleavage before it found its way
back to her face.

'Don't look now,' she murmured, 'but there's
someone over by the railing with their camera
out. I think they're taking a photo of us.'

Of course, he looked. And then he waved. Because that was the sort of irritating man he was.

'I said don't look,' she grumbled.

'Ah, but if I don't look, how can I be sure
they've caught my best side?' Theo asked. 'Besides, they're probably the fifth or sixth person
to take photos of us since we got here. I've seen
at least three.'

'Is that including the hen-party selfie you
posed for?'

'Ooh, no, add that one in.'

Celeste shook her head. 'You love this, don't
you?'

Theo shrugged. 'It's just part of the deal. It's
not why I got into it, if that's what you mean.'

'Why did you, then?' she asked, suddenly cu-
rious. 'Did you always want to be a TV star?'

He laughed at that. 'Not a star, no. I suppose…maybe I did do it for the attention, a bit. I just wanted to do something that made people smile, made them stop in their busy lives and have a laugh, perhaps. Plus it was basically the only thing I was qualified for. Smiling and asking people questions like, "Where do you come from?" It's an aristocratic thing.'

His smile was self-deprecating, but somehow Celeste got the impression that he wasn't actually joking.

She wanted to ask him more about that, but she didn't know how. Damon would have; he was the sibling with all the conversational ability. She'd never needed it before.

But now, she wished she'd spent a little more time on it.

Before she'd found a way to phrase her question, Theo had already moved on.

'So. What are we doing this weekend?'

'Together?' Celeste furrowed her brow as she looked at him. 'I'd sort of planned on staying in and working on my book…'

'As fun as that sounds, it's not going to get us seen.' Theo shifted closer still, a conspiratorial smile on his lips. 'Have you seen the press this thing is getting us both? My agent is over the moon.'

'So is mine,' Celeste admitted reluctantly.

'Apparently raising my profile before the producers make a decision about my new show next year is vital, and *this*—' she waved her hand in the tiny space between them, being very careful not to touch any of those wet, firm abs he was showing off '—is doing that nicely.'

'There are still a few people on social media claiming we're faking the whole thing, though.'

'Which we are.'

'Which is why we need a plan to convince people. Starting tonight, and continuing this week.' Theo settled back against the edge of the hot tub, resting one long arm around her shoulder. He was only touching her ever so lightly, but Celeste still had to force her body not to shiver in response. To the rest of the boat—and the all-important cameras—he probably looked as if he were whispering sweet nothings in her ear.

He wasn't.

'I'm filming Monday and Wednesday evenings, and there's a few meetings I need to attend during the weekdays, but there should still be plenty of scope for us to get together and be seen. I'll send you some calendar invitations once I don't need to worry about submerging my smartphone in bubbly water. What have you got on this week?'

Celeste shook her head as she tried to remember. It was hard to focus when Theo's warm voice was rumbling so close to her ear. 'I have to take my brother Christmas shopping on Thursday,' she replied. 'Other than that… I'm mostly just working on my own. Term is over, you see.'

'Ah, your brother. Maybe it's time to meet the family—properly this time. What do you think? Lunch?'

CHAPTER SIX

THEO WAS STARTING to regret his suggestion of lunch with Celeste's brother.

It wasn't just that he was, yet again, sitting alone in a restaurant, being watched by people with camera phones, waiting for Celeste—who was late. Again.

It wasn't even that he'd belatedly realised that an overprotective brother might not be all that keen on his plan to pretend to date Celeste for publicity—although that wasn't making him feel any better about the lunch ahead, he had to admit.

No, his biggest problem was his own motives.

Yes, being seen with Celeste had gone a long way to rehabilitating his reputation: if *she* didn't hate him, it made it slightly harder for everyone else to. There'd even been a couple of pieces about how Tania had moved on very quickly with her new fiancé for someone who'd been supposedly heartbroken and torn up by his abandonment. Oh, there remained a vocal minority complaining about him on social media, but those following his supposed romance with Celeste were happily drowning them out.

And yes, Cerys was thrilled. So thrilled, in fact, she'd told him he could ease up now. Let something else overtake them in the news cycle, until their romance was forgotten and nobody really noticed they hadn't been seen together in months.

Except he'd done the opposite. He'd invited himself to lunch with her brother. Because he'd seen her in that plain, boring swimsuit and known he'd wanted to see more. Not just that; he'd had fun. Real fun, on a fake hot-tub date.

What was it about her that drew him in? Part of it had to be the passion she showed when she talked about history, or anything she was knowledgeable about. But it was more than that. The way she let him see under that prickly exterior sometimes. Or how much fun it was to ease her out of that comfort zone she loved so much. Or even just the simple way she made a decision about how she felt about things based on what she thought, not on what anyone else said.

Whatever it was, Theo was too far into this, and he knew it. He just didn't seem to have any inclination to get out again.

And then there was the text message he'd received from his mother that morning.

Looking forward to seeing you for dinner on Sunday. We understand—from social media, I might add—that there's a new woman in your life. Your father says you should bring her along to see the old pile. Let her know what she's getting into.

He wasn't entirely sure how he was going to persuade Celeste to have Sunday lunch with his parents—or how he'd explain it to them if she didn't come. Or which was the worst of the two outcomes, to be honest.

But he was going to have to worry about it later. The restaurant door swung open and Celeste strode in, flanked by a tall, handsome guy in a dark coat, and a woman Theo hadn't seen before. She had her dark hair clipped back from her face, and wore a sweater dress under her coat. She was pretty, in a curvy, petite way— but his gaze was quickly drawn back to Celeste, slipping out of her white coat to reveal her customary black clothing underneath.

God, she was beautiful.

Her companions paused just inside the door, looking faintly astonished. Apparently, they hadn't been following Celeste's social media mentions lately, then.

Celeste said something to them both that he couldn't make out, then smiled—her painted red lips wide, although Theo could tell even from the distance between them that it wasn't one of her *real* smiles—and headed towards him.

This was it.

Theo stumbled to his feet as they approached, trying to return Celeste's smile. As she reached him, he did what he always did on dates: he embraced her, then pressed a kiss against her mouth.

Oh. Ohhh.

It was only meant to be a quick brush of the lips, maybe only at the corner of her mouth, even. But somehow it was suddenly more. Nothing deep—no tongue, as Cerys always warned him about kisses in public. But still.

Their first kiss.

And suddenly Theo was very sure that there needed to be another. And another. And…

Celeste pulled away after a moment, colour high on her cheeks. Good. At least he wasn't the only one affected by that kiss.

She pulled herself together more quickly than he could though.

'Sweetheart, you remember my brother, Damon? And my best friend, Rachel?' Celeste said, looking meaningfully towards their lunch guests.

Rachel. Celeste's best friend, Rachel. So he was doing lunch with the brother *and* the best friend.

He really hoped they were both in a good mood.

Switching into TV-host mode, Theo turned on his smile and reached out to welcome Rachel with a hug—*without* kiss—and shake Damon's hand. Neither of them looked as if they were about to bite his head off, but they did both look a little baffled by the whole situation.

Theo knew how they felt.

Pulling out Celeste's chair for her, he ensured she was comfortably seated before taking his own place at the table. Across the way, Damon was doing the same for Rachel.

Theo frowned. Had Celeste mentioned that her brother was dating her best friend? He was pretty sure she hadn't. That was weird, right?

But he couldn't worry about that now. He'd already clocked the paparazzi stalker at a table in the corner, thinking he was being surreptitious as he snapped away, taking photos of the four of them destined to be on the front page of every gossip site tomorrow.

The important thing was to make this seem like a perfectly normal lunch. That was all. So he smiled, and he laughed, and he made small talk. He let Damon pick the wine—who, in turn, got Rachel to choose—and shared mouthfuls of his main course with Celeste from his own fork. The latter prompted an odd look from his lunch date, and frankly astonished ones from their companions. But it looked like a real date, and that was all that mattered.

The only concerning part, really, was the feeling in his stomach that it *was* a real date. Because that was how it felt.

And a big part of him wished that it were.

Huh. That was definitely new. And worrying.

Finally, as they polished off the puddings, Theo glanced casually over at that table in the corner, not for the first time since they'd started eating, and realised that the photographer had left at last.

Leaning around Celeste to peer out of the window, Theo watched the guy wandering off down the London street, waiting until he was around the corner before he collapsed back into his seat with relief.

'He's gone?' Celeste asked, shifting her chair away from Theo's to a more normal distance. Ridiculously, he missed her immediately.

Theo nodded. 'Finally.'

Across the table, Rachel frowned. 'Who's gone?'

'Our reporter-stalker,' Theo said tiredly.

'Come on, let's grab after-dinner drinks in the back bar, where it's more private. Then we can explain.'

The back bar was cosy, warm and empty. Theo spoke briefly to the head waiter on their way in, and he nodded, then shut the door behind them, returning moments later to enter, after knocking, with a tray of coffees and liquors. Then he departed again, leaving them in peace.

Finally.

Celeste sank into a chair a strategic distance away from Theo, and tried to think.

She needed to get things straight in her head again because that lunch had felt uncomfortably like a real date. Not just lunch; hugging Theo hello—*kissing* him even—had felt normal. Natural. Even eating his food from his fork had been fine, despite the fact it was something she'd never even done with her last boyfriend, and they'd been together for almost a year.

She knew it was all fake, of course—intellectually. Knowing things intellectually had never been a problem for her.

It was the emotional side that stymied her, every time. And after a week and a half of pretending to date Theo Montgomery…her emotions were starting to scream at her.

Maybe it wasn't her emotions. Maybe it was

just her libido. *That* at least would make sense. He was an attractive guy. She was a sexual being. Didn't everything in history always come down to sex, one way or another?

Glancing up, she found her little brother glaring at her, and promptly decided to stop thinking about sex.

'What the hell is going on here?' Damon demanded.

Wish I knew, brother.

Rachel sat down beside her, and Celeste heard the unspoken message her best friend was sending.

I might have come here with him, but I'm on your side. Always.

That was something. She'd been…worried, to say the least, talking to Damon about Rachel as they'd shopped for Christmas presents for their parents that morning. And seeing them together at the Cressingham Arcade where they were both currently working hadn't made her concern lessen any.

She'd tried to talk to Rachel about Theo that week, but her friend had ducked her calls—probably, Celeste suspected, because she was in bed with Damon. In a way, she'd almost been glad when Rachel hadn't answered because, really, what was she going to say?

At least she'd shamed Damon into inviting

Rachel to their parents' Christmas Eve party. That was the least he could do.

And he was still waiting for an answer to his question.

'Do you want to explain, or shall I?' Theo asked Celeste, his upper-class tone lazy. That had irritated her a few days ago—the laziness, more than anything. It should irritate her now.

'I'll do it,' Celeste replied, sharply, pushing the thought aside. 'You'll get it wrong.'

'Probably,' Theo agreed easily. He was just *so* laid-back. That was annoying, wasn't it? She was sure it used to be annoying. 'I'll pour the coffees, then.'

She tried to focus on the matter at hand: explaining her relationship with Theo. Maybe it would even start to make sense to her, too.

'So. Damon, I know you watched the car crash that was our festive TV quiz. Rachel, I assume you did too?'

Rachel nodded.

'It didn't go down particularly well with the Internet fans. Or my agent,' Theo said.

Celeste shot him a look to say, *Who is telling this story, you or me?* Theo shut up and let her continue. *One point in his favour. Still so many against.*

Except it was getting harder to remember those points against, when everything felt so natural when she was with him. So easy, in a way personal interactions rarely were for her.

'So Theo called me and asked me to help him rehabilitate his reputation,' she said.

'And yours,' Theo interjected.

Celeste rolled her eyes. 'My reputation is based on my research, my publications, my education and my brain, not my ability to be pleasant on television. Unlike yours.'

'Your reputation with TV companies, however, is based *entirely* on that,' Theo pointed out, apparently unruffled by the accusation that he was just a pretty face.

Celeste ignored him. Mostly because he was right.

'So what happened next?' Rachel asked, obviously well aware of how Damon was glowering at them both.

'We agreed to a few public appearances together, as friends,' Celeste said, trying her hardest to make it sound as if it were the most normal thing in the world.

'It got a little bit out of hand from there,' Theo admitted. 'There were these stories online…'

'People thought we were faking it,' Celeste explained.

'Which you were.' Damon was still glowering as he spoke.

'So we had to prove that we really *were* okay

with each other,' Celeste went on, ignoring her brother. 'By pretending we were in love.'

'So you're mortal enemies pretending to sleep together for the cameras,' Damon said drily. 'The miracle of modern love, huh?'

'Like you can talk,' Celeste scoffed, then turned to Theo. 'This one spent all morning telling me how he and Rachel are just colleagues who sleep together. Apparently, they're having a "festive fling".'

She regretted the words the moment they left her mouth. Of course, that was *exactly* what Damon had said, but, watching Rachel's face as her smile stiffened and the light in her eyes seemed to dim, she knew it was a mistake.

'Sorry, Rachel, that came out wrong,' she said, wincing.

'No, it's true.' Rachel reached for her liquor. Never a good sign. 'He's my festive fling. Right, Damon?'

'Right,' Damon said, although he sounded just as dubious as he had that morning when he'd said it.

Oh, Damon. Oh, Rachel.

She couldn't get her best friend out of this one, or her brother, either. They'd have to figure it out themselves. *She* couldn't even figure out what the hell *she* was doing, pretending to be in love with Theo Montgomery until it almost felt real.

But Celeste had a feeling there were going to be a lot of broken hearts, come the new year.

Theo didn't know what was going on with Damon and Rachel but, to be honest, he wasn't totally sure he *wanted* to know, either. Things were confusing enough to deal with just pretending to date Celeste.

'What do you want to do now?' he asked her as they strolled out of the restaurant together. Damon and Rachel had left, their stalker cameraman had got all he needed, and, really, it was the perfect time for them both to get back to their regularly scheduled lives.

Except he didn't want to. He wanted to spend more time with Celeste. And Theo was almost certain that was going to become a problem, sooner or later.

'Isn't there somewhere we need to be seen together?' Celeste asked.

Every other night, he'd managed to find some sort of event or place he'd been invited to, and convinced her to make an appearance with him for the publicity. Today, for the first time, he had nowhere he was supposed to be, and no ideas.

Celeste rested her head against his shoulder

for a second, as if the rigmarole of the lunch had exhausted her. She had her arm looped through his, close against his side, and Theo had an overwhelming need to keep her there.

It was that thought that sparked the idea.

'Ice skating.' It was perfect; he could hold onto her, in public, with perfect justification.

Celeste, however, looked sceptical. 'We're going back to Winter Wonderland?'

Theo shook his head. 'There's a rink at the Tower of London—well, in the dry moat anyway. Come on. It'll be fun!'

'I do like the Tower,' Celeste said tentatively, and he knew he'd got her. History always was the way to her heart.

Not that he was trying to get there. That was absolutely not what this was about.

He just…needed to hold her close. Was that so bad?

There was a queue at the box office when they arrived. He probably could have used his smile and his face to get to the front of it, but he didn't. Whatever Celeste thought, this wasn't actually another publicity date. This was about spending time with her, like a normal couple.

Even if they categorically weren't.

Did she even *like* spending time with him? He had no way of telling. She was the one person in his life he couldn't read. Everyone else was easy—even Damon and Rachel had been obvious in their own way. He wondered if Celeste realised how much trouble there was going to be there, very soon...

But he wasn't thinking about them. He was thinking about Celeste—which seemed to be one of the few non-work things he *did* think about these days.

He'd never imagined, after their first meeting, that he'd enjoy her company so much. And, in fairness, she was still blunt and impatient, and had given him a real earful the one time he'd called and interrupted her train of thought *just* when she was getting a handle on the chapter she was writing.

But she was also fascinating, full of facts and observations he'd never have imagined if he hadn't met her. There was a passion there he so rarely saw in anybody—one he suspected she only showed when she was talking about history, or perhaps about the things that mattered to her most. He loved listening to her talk— when she wasn't snapping at him. And he loved to watch her think.

Like now, standing in the queue at the Tower of London ice rink, as she stared up at the majestic castle. Her dark hair was swept back from her face as usual, giving him the perfect view of her porcelain skin and the thoughtful look in her eyes.

He couldn't resist. 'What are you thinking about?'

'Do you know, there's been a fortress here since just after the Norman conquest?'

'I did, actually.' She looked at him in surprise, and he shrugged. 'School trip.' It was a lie. He'd come here on his own, as an adult, and read the guidebook cover to cover. Why didn't he just tell her that?

He knew the answer to that too, deep down. Because he was afraid. Afraid that this highly educated woman would laugh at his pretensions to knowledge. What did he know, really? He'd flunked out of university and made his career in a field that just required him to smile and look pretty.

Theo shook the thought away. 'It was a prison too, right? Weren't the Kray twins held here?'

'They were, actually. The last execution here was during the war though—a German spy.' Her smile turned mischievous, and Theo felt his heart skip a beat at the sight. Oh, he was in trouble.

'They say the place is haunted, you know,' she said, and Theo laughed with surprise.

'You believe in ghosts?' he asked incredulously. She was so logical, so academic—so determined to see the evidence and the proof that she'd required dozens of social media screenshots from him to even believe that people were interested in their relationship.

Celeste shrugged. 'Not really. But the stories are always interesting—and the people who claim to have seen them sound terrified. One of them is said to be a grizzly bear, from when the Tower was a zoo.'

'Well, if we see a bear out on the ice, I promise we'll skate in the opposite direction,' Theo said. 'Come on, we're up.'

Celeste bit down on her lip, obviously nervous, as Theo stepped out onto the ice a short while later. He held out a hand to her and she took it, gingerly.

'You've not done this before,' he remembered.

Celeste shook her head. 'Never.'

'Because you didn't want to, or...' He trailed off. If she genuinely hated the idea of ice skating she'd have said, right? He didn't want to be that jerk who dragged her into doing something she didn't want to, just because he thought it would be romantic. Especially since any romance between them was all for show anyway.

'It just...never really came up as an option.' She shrugged. 'My parents weren't big on non-academic activities. And by the time I left home and went to university, well, I was usually busy studying anyway.'

There was something in her voice, a loneliness Theo hadn't heard from her before, and it made his heart ache. She'd been locked away in her ivory tower, learning every dry fact and opinion she could. But when had she actually experienced the world she was learning the history of? He got the impression, not nearly as much as she should have.

'Come on.' He squeezed her hand and led her slowly out onto the ice. 'Don't worry. I won't let go.'

He could have got her one of the plastic penguins kids used when they were learning to skate, he supposed, but he got the feeling that Celeste hated looking incompetent or unknowledgeable as much as he did. But where he laughed his inferiority off and pretended not to care, she got prickly and defensive. He didn't want that. So instead, he kept her close against him and held her up when she started to lose her balance.

They made their wobbly way around the outside of the rink, ignoring the people watching from the cafe and bar at the end, hot chocolates in hand.

'See?' Theo said. 'I told you you could do it.'

Celeste beamed up at him. Unfortunately,

she also stopped focussing on her feet, and her skates slid away underneath her. Theo grabbed her and tried to keep her upright. His stomach lurched as he felt his blades sliding, too. He could grab for the edge, but that would mean letting go of Celeste—

They both crashed to the ice with a jarring crunch.

'I knew I should have used a penguin,' Celeste said, staring up at the night sky above them.

'I reckon it would have been harder to land on than I am,' Theo pointed out from underneath her.

'True.' She looked over at him and he was amazed to realise she was still smiling.

'You don't mind that you fell?'

She blinked. 'I…guess not. I mean, it was fun, even if I wasn't very good at it.'

'It was fun,' he agreed, looking into her eyes and wondering at their depths.

For a long moment, Celeste stared back. Then she blinked and said, 'Come on. I think we deserve a hot chocolate.'

'I reckon they agree.' Theo nodded towards the crowd that had gathered at the side of the rink nearby, all clapping and cheering.

Celeste froze for a moment, then relaxed as she said, 'They recognise you.'

'And probably you.' Theo levered himself out from under Celeste, and back to a standing position. Then he reached down to pull her up beside him, bracing himself against the side of the rink.

One arm wrapped around her waist, he bowed to their audience, pulling Celeste down with him, laughing as she did the same. He liked her like this. Close and carefree. Not caring that she looked like an idiot.

He cared, of course he did. But he knew that the best way to deal with it was to pretend that he *didn't* care. That, and a little bit of distraction…

Swooping around, he swept Celeste into his arms, so her breasts were pressed against his chest, and her skates were barely touching the ice. God, he hoped he didn't fall again now. That really *would* be humiliating.

'What are you doing?' she asked, her voice a low murmur.

'Giving our audience what they really want,' he replied.

Lowering his lips to hers, Theo finally did what he'd been wanting to do since the moment they met at the restaurant, and kissed her. Properly, this time. With tongue.

Somewhere, Theo decided, as whoops went

up from the crowd and cameras flashed, Cerys would be having an apoplexy.

Then he lost the ability to think about anything at all except kissing Celeste.

He didn't miss it.

CHAPTER SEVEN

THEO MONTGOMERY WAS kissing her.

Not like that perfunctory hello kiss at the restaurant; this was a real, no-holds-barred kiss. The sort that would *definitely* send her sprawling over the ice again if he weren't holding her up. Since that brief, hello kiss at the restaurant had scrambled her brains for a good half an hour, she dreaded to think what this one would do.

It's all for show. Remember that. He's just playing up to his audience.

But it *felt* real. That was the problem.

The aches and bruises that covered her body from her fall were rapidly being replaced by other, far more pleasant, sensations. Tingly ones, that reminded her it had been far, far too long since she'd had anyone but herself to keep her company at night. Warm ones, that drove away the chill of a winter night. Hopeful ones, that never wanted these other feelings to end…

Theo pulled away, and Celeste just about resisted the urge to grab his head and pull his mouth back to hers. Mostly because if she let go of his body even for a moment she was pretty sure she was going to fall over again.

The crowd gave up one last, loud cheer, and then dispersed.

'Hot chocolate?' Theo asked, as if nothing had happened at all. As if he hadn't just rocked the foundations of her happy, solitary life by reminding her of all the good things that happened in pairs.

And no, she wasn't talking about the ice skating.

'That would be great,' she managed. 'And I think I'd like my real shoes back, please.'

She needed solid ground under her feet again. Literally *and* metaphorically.

The bar and cafe at the end of the rink were packed with people, but Theo managed to smile their way to a window seat just as another couple were leaving. He disappeared, leaving her looking out over the ice and the castle alone, until he returned with their hot chocolates. It was enough time, at least, for Celeste to bring her brain back down to earth, which she appreciated.

'So, how did you like your first ice-skating experience?' Theo placed her steaming mug, topped with whipped cream, a flake, *and* mini marshmallows, on the counter in front of her.

Celeste beamed at the sickly sweet concoction. Hot chocolate was, in her opinion, the best part of the festive season.

'Worth it for this,' she answered, because she wasn't about to tell him that the *other* best part of this particular festive season was kissing him.

All a show, she reminded herself. She really couldn't afford to forget that.

They drank their hot chocolates in companionable silence as, outside, visitors spun around the rink on their skates, all in the shadow of the ancient castle looming above them. Even Celeste had to admit it was pretty magical.

'You're thinking again,' Theo said, his voice low and rumbly and incredibly distracting. 'More ghost stories about the tower?'

Celeste shook her head. 'I was just thinking how nice it is to see the modern world interacting with history this way. I didn't think it would be, somehow.' She'd assumed that using historical places this way would diminish them, somehow. Probably because of a lifetime of her parents stressing the value and importance of historic and archaeological sites in their own right, for research and learning, for academics who would publish long, often boring papers on them.

And they *were* important, of course. Those historical sources and places were how she'd built her career. She wanted them to be treasured and looked after.

But she wondered now if they couldn't be used, too. Tourists traipsing over the Acropolis in Greece might not do much to preserve it or improve the experts' knowledge of the ancient world. But they *would* increase those tourists' knowledge. And they'd share that knowledge with their kids, their families.

Her father might grumble as another historic site opened its doors to people who hadn't studied the period as he had, didn't understand what they were seeing. He might claim it was all for the money, but the money was what paid for the research to happen.

More importantly, the interest had to be there. If people didn't care about the history of a place, why would they pay for it to be preserved and studied?

All stuff she'd known academically. But here, watching history meld happily with the modern world, she felt that she understood it, rather than just knowing.

There was the world of difference.

This is what I want to do with my TV show. Bring history to life.

'I like it,' Theo said, simply. 'I like that our

city has such a fascinating past, and I like most that it's not locked away there. That we can see it, experience it every day, just living here.'

She'd lived in London her whole life, but she wasn't sure she'd ever just enjoyed the place. She'd either been studying *or* living. Never both at the same time.

She thought she might want to, though. With Theo.

'I think…this is what I want my new show to be,' she said, slowly. 'A way of bringing history beside the modern day. Of making it real to people, not abstract.'

That was the part her parents didn't, couldn't understand. For them, it was another world— one they'd rather live in than this one.

But Celeste wanted both. She just hadn't realised it until now.

'I think that sounds brilliant,' Theo said. 'I can't wait to watch it.'

'If they commission it,' Celeste replied. 'It's still not a sure thing.'

'Ah, Aesop's chickens, huh?' Theo grinned. 'Not counting them before they hatch.'

'That's right.' She tilted her head as she studied him, a surprising thought coalescing in her brain.

'What?' he asked, his expression suddenly nervous.

'Tell me the truth. You're a bit of a history buff, aren't you?'

His gaze slid away from hers. 'It's an interesting topic. I'm interested in lots of things.'

Celeste knew she couldn't read Theo the way she read Rachel, or even Damon. But she was starting to get a feel for him—and not just in the kissing way. There was something more here. He couldn't fake his way out of this, not with her.

'You'd heard me on history shows on the radio often enough to ask me onto that quiz show.'

'I thought you'd be an interesting addition.' He tossed her a smirk. 'Look how right I was.'

'Did you really come on a school trip to the Tower of London?'

Theo paused for a second, then shook his head. 'No. I came as a tourist last summer.'

'Because you're a history buff.'

'Because I was writing an essay about it for my history degree.'

Celeste blinked. Okay, maybe she couldn't read him at all, because she definitely hadn't seen that one coming.

'You're studying history?' she asked.

'Part-time.' He shrugged. 'It's no big deal.'

But it was, she could see that in the tension of his shoulders, the way he wouldn't look at her.

This was Theo behind the smile, behind the fakery.

'Does anyone else know you're doing it?'

His gaze shot up to meet hers at that. 'No. And… I'd appreciate it…'

'I won't tell anyone.' She smiled. 'But I think it's wonderful.'

'You do? For all you know I could be rubbish at it.'

Celeste had had rubbish students before. Ones who didn't show up for lectures, or never turned in essays. Ones who only cared about the university experience, not the studying.

If Theo was doing this in his own time, on top of a full-time job, when he really didn't have to…he was doing it for the love of the subject.

And *that* she most definitely understood.

She smiled at him, and lifted her half-empty mug for him to toast with his own.

'What are we toasting to?' he asked.

'To you, and your studies.'

'How about to you, and your new show?' he countered.

'Fine. To bringing history to life, and into the present.'

'Works for me.' He drank, leaving a hot chocolate moustache on his upper lip, which he licked off. Celeste tried to pretend that the action didn't make her heat up again.

'Now,' he said, when he'd finished. 'Important question for you. How do you feel about Sunday lunch with my parents?'

It was hard for Theo to express quite how much he didn't want to be here. From the way Celeste was watching him, though, her bottom lip caught between her teeth, he had a feeling she understood, at least a little.

Taking a breath, he opened the door of the car. 'Ready?'

'As I'll ever be,' she joked, but he could barely bring himself to smile in return.

Why had he done this? The only thing he could think was that the kiss on the rink had addled his brain to the point where he'd not only told her he was studying history, for heaven's sake, but also forgotten all the perfectly good reasons why he *shouldn't* take Celeste to meet his parents.

Starting with, if *he* didn't want to be there, why should she?

But it was more than that, of course. While he had no doubt his parents would be nice enough to Celeste, he couldn't hope to say the same about how they'd be towards him.

Still, he forced himself not to actively grimace as he helped Celeste out of the car and took her arm. Her dark hair was down today, for once, and it moved in the winter breeze before settling on her white coat.

Any other woman of his acquaintance, coming to meet his parents for the first time, would have asked him what to wear. Not Celeste. He had no doubt that under that coat was an all-black outfit—although a dress or skirt rather than jeans, given the tights she was wearing with her boots today. Her lips were bright red, like Snow White's, and he wanted to kiss them. For courage, perhaps.

Or just because he'd been dreaming of them since he last touched them with his own.

Celeste stared up at Sorrelton House, its many chimneys jutting up into the grey winter sky. 'This is where you grew up?'

Theo tried to imagine seeing the place for the first time. He couldn't remember when he had, of course. He'd been born within its walls, and some days it felt as if he'd never left.

It was a large house. No, that was an understatement. It was unnecessarily huge, for the three of them living there when he was a child, and for his two parents now. Even if he added the live-in staff, which was down to only a few long-standing employees, it was too big. He remembered them closing up the East Wing when he was a child; he didn't think it had ever been opened up again since.

'Yep,' he said, succinctly. 'Come on.'

It was because they didn't have a real title, he supposed, that his parents insisted on all the grandeur. They were minor, minor aristocracy, but even that small amount made a difference. They couldn't live like *ordinary* people, could they? But they didn't have the land or inheritances to live like lords, either.

Theo wasn't sure anyone could afford to live at Sorrelton House these days, the way it had been designed to be lived in. After so many years, the place was a complete money pit.

He didn't bother ringing the doorbell; it would only risk giving Jenkins a heart attack, and it took him forever to get up to the main door from the kitchen, where he spent most of his time gossiping with Mrs Harrow. So instead, he led Celeste around to the side entrance, the one nearest the stables, and slipped in that way. At least he knew that Celeste wouldn't be the least bit interested in the pomp and circumstance of the main entrance hall anyway.

Except in her very own Celeste-like way, of course.

'It's Georgian, right?' she asked, pausing to examine the brickwork as they rounded the corner to the side entrance.

'I believe so.' His voice sounded tight, even

to his own ears. Celeste didn't seem to hear it, though.

'Do you know much about the history of the place? Before your family came here, I mean?' She paused. 'Unless it's *always* been in the family? Are you one of those families?'

'No. My great-grandfather bought it, I believe. Before that, I'm not sure. I imagine my father could tell you, if you really want to know.'

He didn't—want to know, that was. He never had—not since he was a child. His father had made clear that the house was a responsibility, and obligation—one he never expected Theo to be capable of fulfilling to his satisfaction.

So, no. He didn't want to know about the history of Sorrelton House. He wanted to get through this lunch and get back out again, as smoothly and as quickly as possible. That was all.

Celeste was watching him now, curiosity and maybe even concern in her eyes. Theo turned away, fumbled open the door and strode into the house proper. If he moved fast enough, maybe the memories wouldn't hit him so hard.

'Theo? Is that you?' His mother's voice echoed down the empty hallways; she might be getting older, but her hearing was still as sharp as it had ever been. Maria Montgomery had always been able to hear a whispered insult or a secret from a good hundred yards. Apparently, it was still her super power.

'Yes, we're here, Mother.'

Reaching out blindly behind him, he somehow found Celeste's hand and gripped it firmly in his own. They'd agreed on the drive out of London how they'd play this. A new couple, yes, but nothing serious. He didn't want his parents getting any ideas about marriage or anything—not least, because he knew that Celeste wouldn't be their first choice for him. Or second or third, come to that.

After all, she was only beautiful, intelligent, funny and, against the odds, mostly a nice person.

'Where's the money, Theo? Or at least a title? Come on, boy, try harder. That was always your problem—you just never tried hard enough.'

He could almost hear his father saying the words in his head.

Really, what was the point of coming home to be berated by him, when he could do it perfectly well for himself?

'There you are!' Maria burst into the main hall at the same time Theo and Celeste reached it. 'We were starting to think you'd got lost. Or forgotten.'

'Are we late?' Celeste asked, confused. 'I thought you said one, Theo?' He saw her glance at the grandfather clock, as it chimed quarter to one.

Theo didn't answer. Maria didn't bother either as, of course, they were actually early. Five years ago, maybe he'd have second-guessed himself, thought he'd got the time wrong. He knew better now. But how could Theo explain to Celeste that his mother just liked to start with them at a disadvantage, any way she could?

He should have warned her in the car. Shouldn't have brought her at all. But somehow, when he was away from this place, he always believed that it couldn't be as bad as he remembered. That he was building it up in his head, somehow.

It was only once he returned that he realised the truth of it all.

'Come, come. Your father is already in the dining room, Theo, and you know he doesn't like to be kept waiting.' Maria turned away and bustled down the passageway to the dining room at the back of the house.

'I'm sorry,' Theo whispered as they followed.

'What for?' Celeste asked.

'Everything that happens in this house.' That should probably just about cover it.

He braced himself, and headed for lunch.

Forty minutes later, Celeste had a new respect for Theo Montgomery, and his ability to keep smiling and stay polite in the face of abject rudeness. She'd thought he'd done a good job at being pleasant to her, even after she'd spent their first meetings arguing about everything.

Now she knew his secret. He'd been training for this his whole life.

His father, Francis Montgomery, was easy enough to figure out. Perpetually disappointed by life, as far as she could see, and passing that disappointment onto Theo. He was every historical figure who'd ever lost a kingdom, or power, or influence, and blamed everyone but himself. Even the way Theo passed him the gravy wasn't satisfactory.

It was much easier to understand people when you thought of them as historical figures, she decided. Maybe that was the trick she needed, and hadn't realised until now. Something else Theo had given her.

'*He* dropped out of university, you know,' Francis told Celeste, apropos of nothing, over dessert.

She hadn't known. It had never come up. She wasn't entirely sure why it had come up now. And Theo clearly had no intention of telling them about his current studies, so she wouldn't. 'Well, it doesn't seem to have stopped him,' she said cheerfully.

Really, a dinner at which *she* was the cheerful, pleasant, upbeat one was a definite first. And not a good sign.

She glanced across at Theo, who sat staring sullenly at his syrup sponge pudding and custard. She'd never known him go so long without smiling before.

'I think it was the expectation,' Maria, his mother, said, almost as a secret aside, as if Theo couldn't hear them.

'*I* think he was too stupid,' Francis interjected. Maria ignored him.

'Oxford does come with certain expectations, don't you think?' Maria went on. 'And really, all that pressure on young minds. Some people just aren't cut out for that kind of life, are they? But he so wanted to go… *I* always knew my Theo wasn't really going to set the world aflame. It takes a special something for that, don't you think? And we knew early on that Theo didn't have it. But he's found his niche, and that's something,' she added, sounding doubtful.

'He never wanted to work hard, that was the problem,' Francis opined, leaning back in his chair, wine glass in hand. 'That's what happens when people get everything handed to them on a plate, like Theo has. They don't know how to work for it. Born lazy.'

'Well, Theo does actually have a job,' Celeste

pointed out. She stared at Theo, waiting for him to say something, to defend himself, but he barely even looked up from his pudding. 'I've seen him do it—that's how we met, in fact. He works hard.' She thought of all the meetings and filming he'd had scheduled at odd times that week, all the time spent making sure everything was in place for the *New Year's Eve Spectacular*. All the emails and calls. Theo was properly involved in the projects he took on; he did a lot more than show up and smile, whatever people thought.

Whatever *she'd* thought, before she got to know him.

When you added in his studies, plus his fake dating her, Theo was anything but lazy.

But his parents didn't look convinced.

'And now, of course, he associates with all these women who are only interested in his name, or his money—no offence, of course,' Maria went on.

'None taken,' Celeste lied, her voice mild. *That*, at least, made Theo look up and give her a tight smile. She wondered when he'd learned to read her so well.

Maybe around the time she'd learned to read him.

His mother was a harder read—but Celeste was pretty sure she was toxic, one way or another. She reminded her of Rachel's stepmother, the few times they'd met, and that was *definitely* not a good thing. Maybe it was just living with Francis that had soured her, until she couldn't find a good thing to say about her own son.

'I always tell him to bring them home to see the old place,' Francis said, with a wheezy laugh. 'That'll put them off! He can't afford to marry a poor girl, not unless she's at least got a decent title they can trade on.'

There was an awkward pause. Were they really waiting for her to tell them if she had money and/or an aristocratic family?

'Of course, he never does bring anybody home,' Maria said, looking wistfully at Theo. 'I would like to see him settled—with the *right* girl, of course.'

Celeste didn't need the sharp look Theo's mother sent in her direction to get the message there. She might not always be great at reading the subtleties of human nature, mostly through lack of experience, but really, there was no subtlety here.

And Celeste didn't have the patience for death by a thousand insults.

'Well, I think we can all agree that's not going to be me!' Smiling cheerfully, she placed her spoon in her bowl, pushed away the stodgy pudding, and got to her feet, smoothing down her plain black dress. 'And now, I'm afraid, Theo and I really need to get back to London. Don't we, sweetheart?'

'Afraid so.' Were those the first words Theo had spoken since they sat down at the table? 'Sorry, Mum, Father.' He didn't hug them good-bye. She wasn't surprised. The Montgomerys were even less affectionate than her own family, which she hadn't really thought was possible.

'Thanks so much for having me,' Celeste said, as she backed out of the room, because if nothing else she'd managed to learn *some* manners over the last twenty eight years of her life. Even if she wasn't sure these people were really worthy of them.

Neither she nor Theo said anything else until they were in the car, down the driveway and back on the main road again, speeding away from Theo's childhood home.

'Well,' Celeste said, finally.

'I'm sorry.' He sounded so miserable, so tense, that she almost wanted to tell him to pull over so she could kiss him again, just to try and cheer him up.

'It's okay,' she said. 'I mean, it's not. They're awful. But honestly, I'm used to dreadful family dinners, so it was almost nice to sit through someone else's for a change. It's a good job I got to know you first, though.'

'Why's that?'

'Because otherwise I might believe some of the things your parents said about you.' She looked over at him and wished he weren't driving, so he could see the truth of her words in her eyes. 'As it is, I know you're nothing like the man they seem to think you are. So that's good.'

Was that the start of a smile, curving around his lips? She hoped so.

'Nothing like, huh?'

He was fishing for compliments now, but, after meeting his parents, she decided he probably deserved a few. 'Nothing at all. You're definitely not lazy, and you're proving with every essay you submit, every online seminar you attend, that you're capable of studying when you want to.' She'd talked him into showing her some of his modules and marks after a few more drinks after the ice skating. From his online tutor's comments, she could see that he was a conscientious and dedicated student, with interesting opinions and interpretations of events and sources that weren't just a repetition of someone else's analysis.

She almost wished he were one of her students. Except then she definitely wouldn't be able to think about kissing him, so it was probably best for all of them that he wasn't.

He was smiling now. She'd made him smile, just by telling the truth as she saw it. She liked that.

'I'm still sorry you had to sit through that lunch,' Theo said.

'That's okay,' Celeste said cheerfully. 'I know exactly how you can make it up to me.'

He raised an eyebrow at that. 'Oh? How's that?'

'You can come to *my* parents' Christmas Eve party with me.'

CHAPTER EIGHT

SPENDING CHRISTMAS EVE in a room full of people who were categorically proven to be brighter and better educated than him wasn't exactly in Theo's plans when December started. But then, nothing in his life seemed to have gone to plan since he'd met Celeste, so maybe it was all par for the course.

The Hunters' town house in central London was worlds away from his own family seat in most ways, but from the moment they'd arrived Theo had sensed something familiar. Something he didn't like. Celeste, however, seemed perfectly comfortable, so he'd pushed the feeling aside and tried to enjoy the party. She'd been there most of the day, helping prepare for the party, and by the time he arrived—with the obligatory bottle of wine for the hosts, or for himself, in case he got really desperate—there were already half a dozen people milling around the living spaces of the house, including her brother, Damon.

'You okay?' Celeste asked as she drifted past holding a tray of interesting-looking hors d'oeuvres. She was wearing a different dress from the one she'd worn for lunch with his parents a few days before, although it was, obviously, still black. This was cut high in the front but fell low on her back, then swished all the way to the floor, only just revealing that her usual boots had been replaced with high heels.

Theo wanted to pull down the shoulder straps and watch it fall to the floor. Although probably not in the middle of her parents' party, he supposed.

'Fine.' He looked around the room. From the few introductions he'd made, everyone here had several more degrees than him, and mostly wanted to talk about their research with other people who would understand how impressive it was.

He was not that person.

Celeste rested a hand against his arm for a moment. 'Sure?'

She'd been like this since she'd met his parents—more sensitive, more concerned. Less Celeste-like. As if seeing inside his secrets allowed her to drop a little of her own armour. And she was letting him in here, too. Showing him her world.

As if this thing between them *meant* something to her.

Or as if she wanted company at a boring family party. That was the more likely answer.

'I'm feeling…a little out of my depth here,' he admitted reluctantly. He'd worked so hard over the years to fit in anywhere, to win people over, to make them smile in a way he'd never been able to achieve with his own parents. But here…he felt inferior again, just like at home.

He didn't like it.

Celeste reached up and pressed a soft kiss to his cheek. 'Just stay away from my mother and you'll be fine,' she told him.

Well, that was encouraging.

'Keep me company for a few minutes?' he asked, trying not to sound desperate. 'I've barely seen you tonight.'

She flashed him an amused smile. 'You know the people here aren't likely to be posting photos of us on social media, right? Some of them might not even know who you are…'

Theo faked horror at that idea, although actually, right then, it seemed like the better option. He didn't want to be singled out and identified here. Didn't want to be highlighted as the know-nothing TV star.

He wanted to be here as Celeste's date. Nothing more, nothing less.

'That's not why I want to spend time with you.'

'I know! You want my feedback on your latest essay, right?' she guessed. 'I've told you, I'll do it, but only if you give me tips about not appearing scary on television.'

'You don't need them, but I'll give them to you, sure. But not tonight.'

She gave him a speculative look. 'Is it because I've already lectured you on my research and books and you figure I'm the only person in the room who won't bore you again?'

'I'm never bored listening to you.'

'Ah, so it is that,' she said, with a grin. 'In that case, try and avoid my dad, too.'

'Celeste…' She started to move away, and he snaked an arm around her waist to keep her closer. 'Is it so hard to believe I might just want to spend time with you? Because I like doing that?'

The surprise in her eyes hurt, a little. It so obviously hadn't occurred to her that he *might* want to do that—which suggested that she didn't want it.

Then he looked a little closer, as she bit down on her lower lip and met his gaze. '*Do* you? Because generally most people don't.'

'I'm not most people,' he told her. 'And yes. I do.'

A small smile spread across her face, a real

one, one he believed. She opened her mouth to respond—until someone called her name from across the room and, with an apologetic look, she slipped away.

Theo sighed, and reached for another drink. He had a feeling that the evening was going to be a very long one.

An hour later and Theo was still looking pretty miserable. Celeste wished she could stop and stay with him for a while—especially since it seemed he actually *wanted* her company, and not just for appearances—but she had bigger concerns tonight. Mostly around her brother and her best friend. She couldn't afford to be distracted by the thought of kissing Theo again.

However tempting that was.

Her conversations with Damon during the day hadn't made her feel any better about whatever was happening between him and Rachel, although she suspected they couldn't keep pretending it wasn't an issue for very much longer. And Rachel still wasn't here...

Celeste's phone buzzed in her pocket. God, she loved a dress with pockets.

I'm outside. Come meet me?

It was Rachel, of course. Dumping her tray
on the nearest flat surface, Celeste headed for
the door—wincing as she realised that her father
had cornered Theo and looked to be practising
his latest lecture on him. At least Theo was still
managing that polite, TV-star smile. When that
started to slip, that was when she'd worry.

'Why didn't you come in? It's freezing out
here,' she said as she opened the door, looking around for her friend. Then she spotted her,
at the bottom of the steps that led to the town
house's front door.

One look, and she knew. She stared, speech-
less for a moment.

Then, 'Oh, my God, you're in love with my
brother,' she blurted.

'I wanted to speak to you first,' Rachel said,
with a small smile. 'Before I talk to him.'

Oh. Oh, she'd been right. Everything *was*
coming to a head tonight.

Celeste shut the front door behind her and
stepped out into the biting cold of the December night. Descending the steps carefully in her
heels, she sat on the second from the bottom one
in the freezing cold with her best friend.

'Tell me everything,' she said.

And Rachel did.

Some of it she already knew from her conversations with Damon, or the double-fake-date lunch they'd shared. Some of it was new.

And all of it boiled down to one thing—the same thing Celeste had known from the moment she saw her.

Celeste waited until Rachel had run out of steam and words before she spoke.

'So like I said, you're in love with my brother? Is that right?'

Rachel nodded. 'And I'm hoping he feels the same about me.'

Celeste thought back to her last conversation with Damon, in the kitchen before the party started. He'd seemed…conflicted.

'I think he does,' she said slowly. 'The thing will be getting him to admit it.'

She didn't want to give her friend false hope, because her brother was basically a lost cause when it came to love. But on the other hand…

'If anyone can do it, I reckon you can,' she said.

Rachel flashed her a quick grin. 'Do you know, apart from my mother before she died, you were the first person in my life who ever listened to what I had to say without talking over me, or telling me what I should feel. Damon was the second.'

No wonder she'd fallen for him. Celeste knew what a rarity that was in Rachel's life; she'd often assumed that her listening skills were the only reason her best friend put up with her at all. She might not agree with her all the time, and she'd most definitely tell her when she'd got something factually wrong, but she would at least listen first.

'It's one of the most useful things our parents ever taught us,' Celeste said lightly. 'You see, you can't brutally demolish another person's argument or theory without listening to it properly in the first place.'

Rachel laughed, but it sounded more desperate than amused.

'What's he going to say when I tell him?' she asked quietly.

Celeste had no idea. But her friend needed to know the answer, one way or another. 'Let's go and find out.'

Rachel stood up, smoothed down the beautiful wine-red dress Celeste had helped her pick out at the Cressingham Arcade, and nodded.

Inside, the party was still…well, mildly happening, rather than raging. Across the room, Damon stood with their mother, but he turned away from her as Rachel entered, and Celeste almost *felt* the moment his gaze met her friend's.

Whatever Damon told her tonight, it was clear to her that this thing between him and Rachel was no festive fling.

Rachel's heel skidded on the parquet flooring, and Celeste gripped her arm a little tighter, as Theo had hers on the ice rink.

'You okay?' Celeste murmured.

'No.' Rachel held onto Celeste while she found her balance. 'But I will be.'

'Do you want me to come with you to talk to him?' Not that she was sure what she could do, but she could tell her best friend was scared. Rachel was the one person in the world she'd *always* been able to read right. She'd learned her, the same way she learned dates and names and sources. Because from the moment Rachel had become her friend, she'd known she had to work as hard to keep her as she did her grade average.

'No,' Rachel said. 'I need to do this alone.'

'You're sure?'

Rachel's gaze skittered towards Damon, and Celeste's followed. He looked as if he was bracing himself for Sunday lunch with the parents— or, worse, Christmas Day. Maybe he was.

Oh, she had a feeling this was going to go very badly.

'Sure,' Rachel said, sounding more certain than Celeste felt. 'Besides, I need you to do something else for me.'

'Anything,' Celeste said. She couldn't fix this for her friend, but she could help her through it.

'Distract the rest of the room?'

Huh. She hadn't been expecting that, but she supposed it made sense. There weren't so many people at the gathering that any argument between Rachel and Damon would go unnoticed. In fact, it would probably be the most exciting thing that had happened at one of the Hunters' Christmas Eve parties in years. Of course, Rachel wouldn't want a gaping audience—unlike every time she and Theo went out in public.

'Just while I get Damon out of here. I don't want an audience for this,' Rachel went on.

Celeste tried to smile, although she wasn't sure she managed it very well. 'On it.'

She didn't look back as she crossed the room; Rachel had to do this alone now. And she had a job to do.

Unfortunately, the only way she knew to draw the attention of the masses was by kissing Theo Montgomery.

The things she did for her friends…

Celeste's father was obviously a very intelligent man, Theo decided, but he was no storyteller. He'd been talking—at length—about his research and discoveries for the last fifteen minutes, and Theo was still no clearer what he'd actually been doing.

Celeste would have made the story exciting.

He'd have listened to her explain anything. Partly because he was stupidly in thrall to her, but mostly because, despite what she believed about herself, she was actually good at making history interesting. At telling the stories that made the past come to life.

He'd known that about her before he'd even met her, from listening to her on the radio. It was how he knew her new TV show would not only be picked up, but be a success. And it was, now he thought about it, probably why there'd been such uproar after the *Christmas Cracker Cranium Quiz* had aired. People weren't just cross because he'd been mansplaining to her, but because they'd wanted to hear what she had to say, and he'd been following the producer's orders to cut her off.

She'd asked for tips on being on TV but, in truth, she just needed to be herself. She needed to see herself the way *he* saw her—as a passionate, engaged, fascinating historian who made stories of the past feel real and immediate.

He didn't know what her history with men, or other people generally, was like—he hadn't asked and he wouldn't—but he got the impression that others might not have always taken the time to see her that way. Maybe they'd been put off by her sometimes prickly nature—something he suspected now was more down to social nerves than anything else. Or perhaps the people she met simply didn't like being told they were wrong, even when they were.

But she'd let him see beyond the prickles. And he'd been told he was wrong his whole life. It was actually a relief to be told it when it was true. At least Celeste also acknowledged when he was *right*.

She hadn't laughed at the idea of him studying for a degree; she'd encouraged him. And she'd put up with lunch with his parents without flinching, then told him they were wrong about him.

Something he'd been waiting to hear his whole life. Not from fakers like him, who lied for a living.

From someone who told the truth no matter how inconvenient. From Celeste.

And that was why he'd been politely listening to her father drone on for the last thirty minutes, without excusing himself and leaving this travesty of a party. Because if he left, he wouldn't see her again tonight—and, God help him, he wanted to see her again.

He tuned out Jacob Hunter completely as Celeste returned to the room, arm in arm with Rachel—looking stunning in a wine-red gown that had Damon, across the room, standing gawping at her like an idiot. Huh. Obviously things were afoot there.

Suddenly, Celeste broke away from her friend and headed towards him, a determined glint in her eye. Her father didn't seem to have noticed, as he was still continuing a run-on sentence that had been going on for half a glass of wine now. Theo put his glass down on the nearest table, and braced himself for whatever was about to happen.

Celeste grinned. Oh, but he had a bad feeling about this...

She ignored her father as much as Mr Hunter was ignoring her, her gaze not leaving Theo's as she approached. And then she was in front of him, almost pressed up against him, in fact, that slippery black fabric sliding against the front of his freshly pressed shirt.

'Just follow my lead on this one, okay?' she murmured.

And then she kissed him.

It was like the ice rink all over again, with a similar chance of him falling over, just out of shock. Theo froze for less than a second, before the feel of Celeste's mouth on his let his instincts take over, pushing his brain to the back of the queue.

He knew how to do this, whatever her reasons. Hell, he wanted to do this, had been dreaming of doing this, ever since the last time. His baser instincts weren't going to let his brain ruin this for him now.

Around them, there were murmurs, comments, and he happily ignored all of them. If Celeste didn't care what her family and friends were saying about their public display of affection, he sure as hell didn't. Instead, he sank into the kiss, holding her close and wrapping his arms tight around her as if he never intended to let go.

Maybe he didn't.

Celeste, however, had other ideas. Apparently oblivious to the way her kiss was changing his whole world around him, she pulled away, and glanced over her shoulder.

'Okay, they're gone.' She let him go, flashed a smile at her father, and headed out into the hallway.

Theo blinked, then followed.

'What was that about?' he asked as the door to the living space swung shut behind him, and they were alone at last.

'Rachel needed to talk to Damon, without an audience.'

'So you drew the audience's attention our way instead,' Theo surmised.

She smiled. 'Exactly.'

Theo watched her, watched as her smile started to waver. 'Did I do it wrong?'

He laughed, not at her but at himself. 'Sweetheart, trust me. I don't think you know *how* to do it wrong.'

Celeste gave a one-shouldered shrug. 'Oh, you'd be surprised. Guys are generally with me for my brain, or my university connections, rather than my lips or my body. Which, you know, is a good thing, I suppose.' He'd sworn to himself he wouldn't ask about her past romances. It was none of his business—especially since this wasn't even a real relationship. But if she was just telling him, that was okay, right?

'Not if they're just using those parts of you.' He frowned at her. 'Wouldn't you rather have someone who wanted *all* of you? Brains and body, your soul *and* your sexuality?'

Tossing her hair back over her shoulder, Celeste barked her own laugh this time, too sharp and short to contain any actual humour. 'You can talk. You only want me for my publicity.'

God, if only she knew the truth. How much he *did* want her, just as she was. Except for her, this was still about her career, and his. She'd never hinted at wanting anything more. And he could only imagine how people would laugh if he even pretended to be smart enough to have anything more with her. Half a distance-learning degree wasn't going to match up to her PhD and academic credentials any time soon.

But if she honestly thought he wasn't attracted to her, that he didn't dream about her lips, her body under his…then she really hadn't been paying attention.

The question wasn't whether he wanted her. It was whether *she* wanted *him.*

He waited, just a moment, until her gaze settled back on his again. He didn't laugh off her comment the way he would have done before that kiss. Didn't make a joke, and let the moment pass. Didn't hide anything, for once.

He let her see the heat in his eyes. And, because he was watching oh-so-carefully, he saw the answering flare in her own, before she blinked and tried to bury it.

'Celeste.' Theo stepped closer, relieved when she didn't move away. 'Do you really think this is still all about the publicity?'

'Isn't it?' Her tone was defiant, but he heard the hope behind it. 'What else could it be? We had an agreement…'

'And then I kissed you on that ice rink and nearly lost my mind with wanting you.'

A sharp intake of breath was the only response she gave him.

He stepped closer. Her back was already up against the bannister, and he was so close now he could reach past and rest one arm on the wood right beside her head. If she gave him the slightest hint, he'd back away.

But she didn't. That heat was back in her eyes, and he could feel it growing between their bodies, too.

'Celeste, I don't know what this is between us. But it's sure as hell not about the publicity right now, okay? There's no one watching. No cameras. And I still need to do this.'

He ducked his head to capture her mouth with his own, loving the small sigh she gave as their lips touched. She wanted this as much as he did. Needed it, even.

He'd worry about what the hell that meant tomorrow.

It was long moments before he pulled away, panting slightly, and rested his forehead against hers. 'How long do we have to stay at this thing?'

Celeste shook her head, as if she was trying to clear it. 'I told my parents I'd stay here tonight. It's Christmas Eve, Theo.'

He swore. Christmas Eve meant he needed to drive back to Sorrelton House tomorrow morning, to brave the festivities with the family. Christmas Eve meant Celeste would have her own family stuff to do.

'That means I have a bed upstairs,' she

pointed out, and all the blood in his body rushed in one direction.

But before he could sweep her into his arms and carry her up the narrow town-house staircase, Rachel came barrelling through from the kitchen, her face blotchy with tears.

Celeste broke away from him instantly, taking her best friend into her arms and whispering with her. Then she turned back to Theo, her face thunderous.

'Can you get Rachel a taxi, please? I need to go and speak with my brother.'

CHAPTER NINE

HER HEAD STILL swirling from that kiss, Celeste stormed out into the back garden to find Damon.

'I warned him,' she muttered to herself. 'I *told* him to be careful with her heart, and now look. Honestly. *Men.*'

The fact wasn't completely lost on her that she was avoiding thinking about the man she'd just walked away from inside. Had she really been just about to lead Theo Montgomery up to her childhood bedroom and let him seduce her? Or seduce *him* if it came to it?

Yes, her mind replied. And her treacherous body added, *And you still might.*

Focus, Celeste.

She needed to deal with Damon first. Then she could figure out what the hell was going on with Theo.

She found him, eventually, sitting forlornly on the swing at the end of the garden. Her steps faltered for a moment, when she saw how heart-broken he looked.

This is what love does to you. Where lust can lead.

She shook her head. This wasn't about her. And she wasn't Rachel, and Theo wasn't Damon. They both knew what they had was fake. They lived different lives in different worlds that had only intersected for this brief, wonderful time. In the new year, it would all be over, and as long as she remembered that she'd be fine.

'You are the biggest idiot known to man,' she said, sitting down beside him.

'I know.' God, he sounded miserable.

'Let me guess.' Celeste kicked off the floor with one foot, making the old swing seat sway forward and back. 'She asked you to commit and you said no.'

'Basically.'

'Why? Because you wanted to be free to sleep with as many other women as possible?' If that was the case, she was walking out of here right now and leaving him to be miserable on his own.

'No!' The horror in his voice surprised her into silence. 'Because I'm not that guy. I'd let her down, in the end, when she realised that.'

Oh. *Oh, Damon.*

His head was bowed, his hands clasped between his knees, so she saw clearly the moment his spine stiffened, as if someone had walked over his grave.

'Damon?' she asked, concerned.

'I'm okay.' A lie, but she let him have it. If he was having a come-to-Jesus revelation moment, she didn't want to ruin it. Especially if it might just set him on the right path again.

'For what it's worth? I don't think you'd let her down, little brother.' Standing up, she pressed a quick kiss to his hair, something she couldn't remember doing since he was a child. 'In fact, I think you've got a better handle on this love thing than most of us. You just need to be brave enough to go after it.'

She was as surprised by her words as he obviously was, but she knew they were right, deep down. Damon was a good guy, and if he loved Rachel then he'd do everything in his power to make it right.

Celeste headed back up to the house, her head still whirling. The whole thing was just a reminder how distracting and distressing love could be. She'd never been sure if her parents really loved each other, or if their academic goals were just so neatly aligned that they'd decided they might as well team up. Either way, they'd made a good enough go of it, but they weren't exactly role models for affection and romance. Or parenting, come to that.

It seemed she'd spent her whole life trying to prove to them that she was as good as they were, earning their love through academic achievements—while Damon had gone the opposite way entirely and followed his own path, never trying to impress anyone at all, never committing to anything.

Celeste had already heard her mother's opinion about her choice of date for the evening; she imagined that it was probably about as favourable as Theo's parents on her. She didn't have a title or money. And Theo didn't have a PhD or a research grant or publishing history. He didn't even have an Oxbridge degree, it turned out.

She reached the back door and stared through the kitchen to where Theo was standing in the hallway, alone. He leaned against the bannister where he'd kissed her, running his hand through his hair. Was he having the same second and third thoughts as she was? Probably.

They weren't a match, that much was clear. But did they need to be, really?

Only if it's for ever.

And it wasn't. It was just for now. And right now... Celeste's body knew what she wanted, even if her mind was still spinning.

She let the door slam shut behind her, and

Theo looked up instantly, his gaze locking with her own.

'I put Rachel in a cab,' he told her as he moved closer. 'She was heading to the Cressingham Arcade.'

'Good.' If Damon wanted to go after her, he'd find her easily enough there, right? Those two could figure things out on their own from here.

She had her own love life to sort out.

No, not love life.

Her *sex* life. Something that had been dormant for far too long—not a problem that she imagined Theo having. Which meant maybe he could help her get over her drought, with both of them clear that was all this was.

She stepped towards him, closing the gap. 'In that case, where were we?'

Theo's eyes were dark. 'You were telling me about the bedroom you have upstairs. And how it's Christmas Eve.'

The way he looked at her, she felt like his Christmas gift, waiting to be unwrapped.

Maybe she was.

Do I really know what I'm doing here?

No, she admitted to herself. She hadn't got a clue. But she'd lived her whole life so far knowing exactly where she was going—which degree, which research project, which professor she wanted to study under.

Perhaps it was time to take a leap into the unknown, for a change.

In the other room, she heard her mother laugh, and her father clink some silverware against a glass, ready to make his customary Christmas Eve speech. She didn't need to hear it to know it would be the same as the year before, and the year before that.

She was ready for something new.

'Come upstairs with me?' she asked softly.

Theo hesitated, and she almost took back the whole thing. 'Why?' he asked.

Celeste swallowed. But she'd come this far, she wasn't going to stop now. And besides, having a clear overview of her objectives was a positive thing, right? That was what her PhD supervisor had always said anyway.

'Because I want you, and I think you want me. Not just for the publicity, but for the fun of it, too. So I think you should make love to me tonight, because I can't imagine going another minute without kissing you again.'

Theo surged forward at her words, sweeping her into his arms and kissing her the way he'd wanted to all night. She kissed him back, with all the passion she put into the things that mattered to her: history, proving people wrong, and kissing him.

God, he loved a woman who had her priorities in order.

'Upstairs,' he murmured against her lips.

He could hear Celeste's father droning on in the other room, but there was no way his guests were going to put up with that for very long, and he wanted to be secluded away in her bedroom before any of them escaped out to the kitchen and found them half naked.

Because he was going to have Celeste half naked—no, totally naked—very soon, wherever they happened to be at the time.

'Yes,' she gasped back. 'Upstairs.' She looked back through the door into the garden. He followed her gaze, and saw a figure approaching in the darkness. 'And fast, before my brother gets here.'

They ascended the narrow staircase together, still touching and kissing at every step, hiding their ebullient laughter as Damon stormed through the hallway below and straight out of the front door. And then they were at a dark wooden door, and it was opening, and all Theo could see was a bed and Celeste, and suddenly the laughter faded.

'You're sure about this?' he asked softly, wanting her to know she could change her mind, at any point.

But she nodded, firmly. 'Very.' She bit down

on her lower lip for a moment, the telephone-box-red lipstick she'd been wearing almost all gone now, probably smeared across his face.

He kicked the door shut behind him and swept her up into his arms.

Theo wanted to take it slow, to make it worth the wait, to make it better than she could imagine. But as with all things, Celeste had her own ideas, too. Not that he was complaining about them.

In no time, his jacket, shirt and tie had been stripped away, and her hands roamed across his chest, followed by her lips. Swallowing the lust that coursed through him at her touch, he pushed the straps of her dress down her arms, kissing every inch of creamy skin as it was revealed. Her shoulders, her collarbone, the curve of her breasts…

She arched against him, pressing her softness up against all the parts of his body that were anything *but* soft right now, and Theo almost lost his mind.

'On the bed,' he said, his voice desperate and rasping, even to his own ears.

'Yes,' she replied. Then she grabbed his shoulders and, twisting them around, pushed him down onto the mattress so she landed on top of him.

Theo gazed up at her. Her dark hair was loose around her bare shoulders, tousled and wild. Her eyes were huge in the moonlight, her creamy skin almost glowing as he ran his hands over it, from her shoulders, down her arms, skirting her bare breasts, to where her black dress was pooled around her full hips.

She looked like an ancient goddess—Aphrodite or Venus—come to enchant him. Or a queen, perhaps. Anne Boleyn, seducing her Henry and changing history.

All Theo knew, in that moment, was that whatever she asked for, he would give.

Another time, another place, the thought would terrify him. But right now...

'Are you going to have your wicked way with me?' he asked, the familiar smirk on his lips giving him courage.

This could be just like every other meaningless encounter in his life. Just because it was *Celeste*, didn't mean it had to, well, mean anything.

She grinned down at him, her hair brushing against his chest as she dipped her head to kiss him. 'Definitely.'

'Good.' He grabbed her around the waist and pulled her flush against him as he kissed her again.

He'd worry about everything else in the morning. Right now, he intended to enjoy every minute.

* * *

Celeste awoke on Christmas morning in her childhood bed, with Theo's arm resting heavily on her waist, his breath almost a snore in her ear—and her bedroom door crashing into the wall behind it as Damon and Rachel burst in.

'We're getting married!' they announced, in gleeful unison. Celeste blinked at them. Their eyes seemed feverishly bright with happiness or lack of sleep, their cheeks pink from the cold, and their hands clasped tight together.

Grabbing the sheet to her chest, Celeste struggled to a sitting position, which was harder than it should be since apparently Theo slept like the dead.

She should probably cut the guy some slack. She couldn't exactly blame him for being tired after all their…exertions, the night before. Heat rose to her cheeks at the memory of him declaring it was his turn, after she'd, well, had her wicked way with him, as he put it.

They'd stopped keeping track of whose turn it was, after that, but suffice to say the night had not been exactly *restful*. Thank goodness for solid Victorian walls, and the fact that her parents' bedroom was on the next floor up.

She forced her mind back to the present. The room was still mostly in darkness. If she was lucky, maybe they wouldn't notice that she was naked. Or that she wasn't alone in the bed. It could happen.

Then their words caught up with her.

'Wait. Married?'

She'd hoped her brother and her best friend would be able to sort things out. But *married*? How had Damon gone from a confirmed commitment-phobe to a husband-to-be in just one night? That seemed a lot to chalk up to Christmas magic.

But perhaps that same magic was responsible for what had happened with Theo, too. Because in the cold morning light it seemed more like an impossibility than ever. Apart from the bit where he was still snoring in her bed beside her.

Damon shrugged. 'We just figured…once you know you want to spend your life with another person, why wait?'

'Plus, you had to come up with something really good to make up for being such an arsehole,' Celeste said, reading between the lines.

Rachel thrust her left hand towards her, showcasing a glittering diamond. 'You get to be maid of honour, of course. And you can't wear black.'

'Black is very chic for bridesmaids these days,' Celeste said automatically, with no idea at all if it was true.

'I'm more worried about the "maid" part,'

Damon said, a small frown appearing between his eyebrows—yet still utterly failing to completely hide his happy glow—as he gazed past her to the lump under the sheets beside her.

Celeste rolled her eyes. 'Little brother, my sex life is none of your business.'

Of course, Theo chose that moment to wake up, rolling over languidly onto his back before sitting up, his chest bare as he rested against the headboard.

'Merry Christmas, everybody. What did I miss?'

'Damon and Rachel are getting married, and you and I are having the most awkward morning after known to history.'

'And you know history,' Theo replied. 'Congratulations, guys. Damon, I'd shake your hand, but I'm not entirely sure where my trousers are.'

'I think they're over by the window.' Rachel squinted in the semi-darkness of the room. 'I can see the belt buckle shining in the moonlight.'

'How romantic,' Damon said drily. 'So, you've heard our news. Care to fill us in on yours?'

'No news!' Celeste said brightly. 'Just, you know, carrying on the charade that Theo and I are madly in love and together. All for show.'

'Except you're both naked under there.'

Damon did not look entirely pleased at the idea. She supposed she didn't blame him. She had made it very clear that there was nothing real between her and Theo, and the guy did have a bit of a reputation. Celeste frowned. Except so did Damon, and his relationship with Rachel had been equally iffy to start with. Her brother had literally no moral high ground to stand on.

Plus, as she'd already pointed out, her sex life was none of his business.

Rachel, thankfully, was slightly more subtle than her new fiancé. 'Anyway, we just wanted to share our news…'

'You don't know that we're naked. We could have clothes on,' Celeste said, because apparently she just didn't know when to stop digging. Beside her, Theo was smirking. She could feel it.

'I can see your underwear hanging from the wardrobe door handle,' Damon replied.

'And now we'd better go and tell the rest of our families,' Rachel said, bundling Damon towards the door again. 'Happy Christmas, you two! See you both later.'

'Merry Christmas,' Celeste called after them. 'And, uh, congratulations!'

The door crashed shut behind them, and then it was just her and Theo.

Naked.

In her bed.

'So, that was an exhilarating way to start the day,' Theo said. 'What do you say we take another nap to get over it? Or something.' His hand crept up her bare side at the 'or something', leaving her in no doubt what he was hoping that something might be.

And she wanted that, too. She could feel her body already starting to respond to his touch, her nipples tightening under the thin sheet that covered them, the ache that pulsed through her. How could she want him this much when, to be fair, she'd already had quite a lot of him last night?

Christmas Eve magic, that was what it had been. And, oh, it had been magical.

But in the cold light of day, this desperate need to touch him left her with more questions than she liked.

Hang on. Cold light of day. Cold, yes, but there still wasn't much light pushing its way around the curtains.

'What time is it?' she asked, pushing his hand away.

Theo grabbed his watch from the nightstand. 'Urgh. Four-thirty. No wonder it still feels like the middle of the night. We should definitely get some more sleep.'

Celeste wriggled back down under the covers.

Maybe if it was still last night, she could enjoy this—enjoy him—a little longer.

Because she knew this couldn't, wouldn't last—that had never been the plan. But maybe it didn't have to be over just yet.

She reached out and ran her hand up *his* side, just as he'd done to her, from thigh to chest, before bringing it back down his front instead. 'Sure about the sleeping part?' she asked.

'Not in the slightest,' Theo replied, and kissed her.

CHAPTER TEN

HE'D DEFINITELY HAD worse Christmas mornings, Theo decided, as he left the Hunter town house a little later that morning, whistling to himself in the cold, still dark air. Yes, he was knackered, and slightly hungover, and certain muscles ached in pleasurable ways after the kind of workout they'd only dreamed of for the last few years, but still. *Definitely* worse mornings.

Celeste had tried to convince him to leave quietly, by the back door preferably, without being seen. He'd given her a look and reminded her that the whole *point* was that he should be seen. This was the perfect addition to the story they were weaving for the press—and it seemed important to remember that this morning. Otherwise, a guy might start to get ideas.

Except there were no press waiting for him outside the town house as he left—although he did bump into Jacob Hunter on the stairs, which was more than a little awkward.

His good mood lasted all through his walk home, while he showered and dressed and loaded the car—taking an extra coffee to keep himself awake on the drive—and right up until he pulled his car into the driveway of Sorrelton House.

Christmas with the family. He'd wish he could have just stayed with Celeste for the day, except then he'd have been spending Christmas with *her* family, which, after last night, he wasn't sure was demonstrably better.

Except he'd have been with Celeste. Touching her. Kissing her. As if they really *were* a couple, and not just pretend.

She'd been quick enough to denounce that anything had changed between them to her brother, but it *had* changed, hadn't it? Surely it had to, after a night like that?

The only question was, what had it changed into? He'd have to wait until he was back in London, back with Celeste, to answer that one.

He killed the engine, but stayed sitting in the car on the driveway for a moment, staring up at Sorrelton House. He wished Celeste could be with him again this time. For all his duty visits to his parents drained him, it had somehow seemed less awful when she was beside him. Not that he imagined she'd be volunteering for another visit any time soon. Just as he wouldn't be attending one of her father's lectures.

Different worlds.

But in some ways they intersected. She didn't laugh at his studies. He didn't tell her she should stick to academia, not TV. She made him think that maybe, just maybe, there really was something more to him than his name and his face, after all. And he hoped he'd shown her last night that he knew she was a hell of a lot more than just a brain and the ability to recite facts.

Although, to be honest, he could sit and listen to her recite facts all day. Because they weren't just facts, just history, when Celeste said them. They were stories, a new way of looking at the world. The way *she* saw the world. And he was a little bit worried that he'd never get enough of that.

Theo sighed, and hoped that her confidence in him might help him make it through Christmas Day with his parents, without him starting to believe everything they said about him again.

He didn't notice the unfamiliar car on the driveway until he'd already dragged his overnight bag and box of gifts up the front step to the main door. He frowned at the vehicle as he waited for the door to be answered; Christmas was, of course, a formal occasion, and he knew he wouldn't be forgiven for using the side entrance on such a day.

Who could possibly be here?

Other than his aunt Gladys, who always joined them for high days and holidays, and perhaps the widowed vicar from the church at the edge of the estate, he couldn't imagine *anyone* choosing to spend Christmas Day at Sorrelton House.

He got his answer quickly enough, however, as the door was yanked open, not by Jenkins, but by a vaguely familiar blonde in a green and red tartan dress. She was a good few years younger than him, as best he could guess, and Theo had the horrible feeling that he really should be able to place her. Especially if she was spending Christmas with his family.

He forced himself to smile instead of frown as he tried to buy time while he figured it out.

'Merry Christmas!' he said cheerfully. 'How are things going here this festive morning?'

The blonde smiled wanly at him. 'Happy Christmas, Theo. It's lovely to see you again.'

She pressed a dry kiss to his cheek, then moved aside to let him enter.

'Ah, the prodigal son returns, eh?'

That voice, Theo recognised. And the portly figure it belonged to, waddling into the hallway. Hugo Howard, his father's long-term friend and sometime business partner. Which meant the blonde had to be his daughter, Emmaline. Theo didn't think he'd seen her since she was about twelve, so he didn't feel quite so bad about not recognising her.

The family tableau was completed as Hugo's wife, Anna, a tall, thin woman who towered over her husband and glared at everything because she refused to wear her glasses and blamed poor inanimate objects for her not being able to see them, joined them.

'Hugo, Anna. Merry Christmas,' Theo repeated. 'Not that it's not lovely to see you all, but are my parents here too?'

Hugo laughed uproariously. 'You always were the funny one, Theo. Like your dad says, at least you found a way to make people laughing at you a good thing. They're through in the green sitting room. Come on, now.'

Theo shook off the only vaguely veiled insult without comment. But what did it say about his presence here that the unexpected Christmas guests were more likely to greet him at the door than his own parents?

'It's a good job I got to know you first, though. Because otherwise I might believe some of the things your parents said about you.'

Celeste's words, after their last visit. She knew him even better now, of course. But even then, even after only a few fake dates and an acquaintance of less than three weeks, she'd seen him more clearly than his own parents had. She'd understood him, in a way he knew now his own family never would. She made him see himself through her eyes—not the TV-viewing public's, or his father's critical gaze. But Celeste's clear, unwavering, uncompromisingly honest view.

And he saw her, too. She was becoming all he ever wanted to see.

He dumped his overnight bag at the foot of the grand staircase and fell into step beside Emmaline as they all headed for the sitting room.

'This is a surprise,' he said amiably. 'Is your joining us today a last-minute thing, or did my parents just forget to tell me again?'

'Fairly last minute, I think,' Emmaline said, with a smile that barely reached her lips, let alone her eyes. 'I think your father called mine last Sunday and asked us to join him. We were supposed to be going to my brother in Hampshire, but…' Shrugging, she trailed off.

Last Sunday. After he'd visited for lunch with Celeste, then. Suddenly, Theo was very suspicious about the presence of his unexpected guests.

'Didn't my mother tell me you were recently engaged?' He glanced down at her ring finger, and found it bare. Ah.

'It got called off.' No smile at all this time, understandably, just a tight, pinched look.

'I'm sorry.'

'No need to be sorry!' Hugo said, from in front of them. 'All for the best, I say. Plenty more fish in the sea, after all, right, Emmie?' He shot his daughter a significant look, then moved his gaze onto Theo.

Right. Of course.

The sequence of events was falling into place perfectly in his head now. He'd brought Celeste to lunch; his parents had been horrified. So, of course, they had to find someone more 'suitable' for him. And who could possibly be more suitable than the recently dumped daughter of his father's richer-than-sin best friend? The Howards had no title, or pretensions to one, but they had a lot of money. While Theo and his family had the cache of being on the fringe of the aristocracy.

He was sure his father would have preferred he marry someone with money *and* a title, but needs must. And they were obviously very set against Celeste.

It almost made him want her more.

But most of all, it made him want to take a stand against his parents. To step outside the toxic circle they surrounded him with whenever they were together. To tell them, finally, that enough was enough.

He was himself. *He* was enough. And he'd fall in love with whoever the hell he wanted, regardless of what they thought about it.

Not that he was in love with Celeste Hunter, of course. But the principle remained.

And for once, Theo didn't think his usual survival tactics of staying silent and trying not to care were going to get him through Christmas Day with the family. Because he saw things differently now. More clearly.

Thanks to Celeste.

'I really am sorry about this,' he murmured to Emmaline as they entered the sitting room.

She shrugged thin shoulders. 'Could be worse,' she said. 'My brother's wife has eight dogs, and only half of them are house-trained. At least I don't need to worry about that here.'

A ringing endorsement of their Christmas, Theo thought.

At least he wasn't standing in dog muck. Yay him.

It wasn't enough for him, any more. He was done being grateful to be part of the family, to have the name and the face that had put him where he was. He was worth more than that. He wasn't a disappointment—not to himself. At least, he *wouldn't* be, if he kept going after the things that mattered to him. He had more to give than just a charming smile and a posh accent. He could do more than marry money or fame.

And he had to tell his parents that. Today.

Celeste's parents were not, by nature, early risers. But since Damon and Rachel appeared to be fuelled solely by love that Christmas morning, by the time she'd shooed Theo out the front door and ventured into the kitchen in search of coffee, it seemed the whole house were up and ready for the day.

They were also all staring at her.

'What?' Did she have her dressing gown on inside out? Or were Theo's pants stuck to it, somehow? She'd thought this morning couldn't get more embarrassing, but she was willing to be proven wrong.

'I met your young man again on the stairs this morning,' her father said, over the rim of his coffee cup. 'He seemed to be leaving in a hurry.'

Celeste winced. 'Well, it's Christmas Day. He had to get back to his own family.' Poor sod. 'Did Damon and Rachel tell you their happy news?'

'They did.' Her mother poured her a cup of coffee—steaming hot and black, no sugar, the way they all took it. Damon joked it was the only thing all four of them actually had in common.

'Are you ready to reconsider the whole black for the maid of honour thing yet?' she asked Rachel. At least if her best friend was marrying in, she'd always have someone on her side in family debates.

Unless Rachel took Damon's side, of course. Hmm, maybe she hadn't thought this through well enough, when she'd encouraged Damon to follow his heart.

Rachel shook her head and turned her attention back to her coffee—milky white and loaded with sugar, just as she'd drunk it at university.

'Celeste, we're worried about you,' Damon said. Her parents nodded in agreement.

Wait. What?

'The three of you are worried about me?' She kind of needed the clarification. After all, she couldn't remember the last time it was Damon and her parents against her, instead of her and their parents against Damon, when it came to family disagreements.

She was the one who did everything her parents expected of her, followed the path they'd walked first, became what they'd hoped for in a child.

But apparently her sleeping with a TV star was where they all drew the line.

'Possibly for different reasons,' Damon said, giving her a look she knew all too well. It was his 'our parents are ridiculous' look. 'But all *four* of us are concerned.'

Oh, God, he was bringing Rachel into it now. He'd be talking about them as a pair *constantly* now, saying 'we think this' or 'we like to do it that way' as if they were so fused together it was impossible for them to have different thoughts or opinions on anything.

She hated it when people did that. She'd never imagined her brother would be one of *them*.

But then, she'd never imagined he'd agree with their parents about anything, but here they were.

'You too?' she asked her best friend.

Rachel gave her an apologetic smile and a small shrug. 'I don't want you to get hurt, that's all.'

Celeste raised her eyebrows. 'Seems to me I was saying the same thing to you not so long ago…'

'The point is, darling, that you need to think seriously about how this looks.' Her mother rested her hands on the kitchen table and looked earnestly at Celeste.

'How it…looks?' Had she just not got enough sleep, or was this really as weird as it felt?

'For your career,' her father put in. 'How it looks to the university.'

'It's bad enough doing those puff pieces for those podcasts.' Diana shook her head at the very idea. 'But doing seasonal novelty television as well—and now cavorting around with that TV presenter, too!'

'Nobody is going to believe that you're serious about your research if you're peddling history-lite to the masses,' Jacob said firmly. 'And really, being seen with That Man is just another sign to everyone that you've made your choice—and it's not the right one.'

Celeste could feel strange emotions bubbling up inside her. Ones she wasn't used to feeling. This went beyond irritation or frustration. Yes, she snapped at people all the time when they interrupted her, and she got frustrated when people wouldn't just see that she was right. But those feelings were nothing like the anger that seared through her now.

'Let me get this straight,' she said, her voice clipped. 'Damon, you and Rachel are concerned because you think I'm going to get my heart broken by a TV heart-throb who is only dating me for the publicity, right?'

'Pretty much,' Damon replied.

'And Mum, Dad. You're worried that I'm sabotaging my academic career by taking on TV projects, and that associating with Theo will affect my position at the university.'

Jacob beamed. 'Exactly! See, Diana, I told you she'd understand.'

Celeste's smile felt wicked on her lips. 'Oh, I understand. I understand that you're all very, very wrong about me. And maybe I've been wrong about you, too.'

She spun towards Rachel and Damon. 'I appreciate your concern, guys, but, trust me, everything is fine. Theo and I have an understanding. This isn't like your festive fling, or whatever. That was always just a stupid excuse for you two to have sex without thinking about the consequences. Theo and I know exactly where we are—and it's not leading to flashy diamond rings on Christmas Eve. He's using me for the publicity, and I'm using him for that too—ready for the new TV show I've signed up to hopefully present next year.' Her mother gasped at that. Celeste didn't turn her head, but out of the corner of her eye she could see Diana resting her head dramatically against Jacob's chest. 'The sex,' she added, for impact, 'is just for fun. Nothing more.'

'Now hold on a moment. What is this about a TV show?' Jacob asked.

Celeste moved to face her parents now. 'And you two. You don't care at all that the guy I'm sleeping with is using me. You don't care about my heart, at all. You're just worried that I might show you guys up on the lecture circuit, that your colleagues will think you produced a light-weight, right?'

'Darling, *we* know you're a perfectly adequate historian,' Diana said.

Behind her, Celeste heard Damon smother a laugh.

Perfectly adequate. That wasn't, surprisingly, the part that got to her. It was the way they thought of her as a historian first. That really was all she was ever going to be to them, wasn't it? Or rather, she mattered more to them as an academic than as their daughter.

Suddenly, she had a feeling she knew how Damon had felt all these years.

She was more than just an academic or historian. She was a storyteller. She could bring history to life and share it with others, help other people to feel the same passion and enthusiasm she felt for the past. Show them how the present, the world they all lived in, was built on events that had happened decades or centuries before. How knowing the *truth* about the past made understanding the present—and the chance of change for the future—possible.

Why it mattered—not just to her, but to society. Theo had shown her that.

'I don't want to talk about the TV show today,' she told them, calmly. 'We're not going to agree on it, I can see that. I believe that history belongs to everyone, and it's important to share it with anyone willing to learn it. I don't want to lock it up in academic texts—I want to live it, to show how it connects with the everyday.'

Her parents stared at her. They didn't get it. She'd known they wouldn't.

She took a deep breath. She'd said her piece about Theo. It was Christmas Day, and Damon and Rachel had just got engaged. And she needed to do a hell of a lot more thinking before she was sure what any of this meant for her future.

But she could see a conversation—no, an argument—with her parents in her future, about her career. And for the first time in her life, she realised that it didn't matter what they wanted or expected from her. She was never going to win their respect the way she'd always dreamt of.

But she could respect herself, and her own achievements. And maybe that would be enough.

'Come on,' she said. 'It's Christmas. Let's… let's just forget all this, just for today. Who wants a Bucks Fizz while we open presents?'

Damon squeezed her shoulder as she headed

for the fridge to find the champagne and orange juice, and Rachel gave her a sympathetic smile.

But it didn't stop Celeste wishing that Theo were there, too.

Christmas Day seemed to go on for ever.

From the strategically placed mistletoe that somehow he and Emmaline kept being directed towards, to the barbed comments at dinner, and the discovery that the Howards would be staying until Boxing Day, Theo was exhausted by the time the clock chimed ten, and his mother yawned for the third time, and he figured he could reasonably excuse himself to bed.

To bed, but not to sleep. He had a call to make, first.

Celeste had never been far from his thoughts that day. In some ways, it had felt as if he were watching the whole scene through her eyes. He could hear her sharp comments and smart observations in the back of his mind, all day long.

Now he wanted to hear them for real.

He made it as far as the stairs before his father caught up to him—a surprise in itself. Normally he preferred to demand that people come to him.

'Theo. Son,' he said, and Theo turned, already on the fourth step, to face him.

'Yes?' Maybe this was a Christmas miracle, after all. Maybe his father was about to tell him he was proud of him—and even if it was all down to the whisky, Theo knew he'd take it.

But, no.

'I hope you appreciate the effort that everyone here has put in today to helping you,' his father said. 'And what you need to do next, in return.'

Theo blinked, slowly. 'I'm sorry?'

'I know you're not the smartest tool in the box but damn it, Theo, I thought even you'd be able to figure this one out.' Francis Montgomery's face grew redder with frustration, as well as alcohol. Theo just watched.

He felt strangely detached from the situation. He could see his mother coming up towards them now, carefully closing the door to the room where the rest of their party sat, to spare them hearing this, he supposed.

'Why don't you tell me, Dad?' His voice was calm, too. Calmer than he'd expected he'd manage. There was none of the energy he displayed on camera, and no smile, either. As if he felt nothing at all. 'What is it, exactly, that you're expecting me to do to win your favour?'

'As if you don't know!' Francis blustered, taking a step up the stairs. 'All you've ever needed to do was bring some sort of good to this family. We weren't expecting much from you, but really! Just marry a girl with money and save the family estate, how hard is that? We even *gave* you the girl today, gave you every opportunity, and you didn't make the smallest effort with her! If we have to sell this estate, it will all be your fault.'

Theo was glad of the calmness that flowed through him, wherever it came from. As his father grew angrier, the calmness only increased, letting him see the man before him more clearly than ever.

'No,' he said simply. 'It won't. *You* couldn't save it, Dad. *You* weren't good enough, not me.'

'Theo, don't you speak to your father that way! He's never said you're not good enough.' An outright lie from his mother. It didn't surprise him. She always liked to rewrite events to suit her own narrative.

But Theo was done believing it.

'I want you both to listen to me, for once,' he said. 'I am not going to marry Emmaline, not least because she doesn't want us to get married any more than I do. In fact, I'm not going to marry anyone just because they have money, or because you approve of them. That's not the world we live in any more, in case you haven't noticed.'

His parents were uncharacteristically silent, so Theo carried on, amazed at how good it felt to say the words at last.

'If you want to save this house, save it. Don't

expect me to do it for you. Because honestly? I'd rather you sell the place anyway.' His mother gasped at that, and his father's face turned an even more extreme shade of puce. But Theo didn't care. Because it was true. He didn't want Sorrelton House and all its memories—especially since so few of them were good ones.

He wanted his own life. His own decisions.

He wanted to find out for himself who he was and what he could achieve—not what his parents had always told him he couldn't.

'I don't need anything from you any more,' he said, feeling the truth of the words as he spoke them. 'Sell the house, do whatever you want with the money—I have my own. I have my own life, my own career, and you know what? I've worked damn hard to get where I am, and I'll keep working for the life that I want. Away from here.'

Then he spun round and jogged up the stairs, whistling a Christmas carol as he went.

He'd leave this place tomorrow, and he wasn't sure he'd ever come back. Wasn't sure he'd be welcome, even if he wanted to.

But that was okay.

He could find his own future now.

Theo changed out of the dinner jacket and bow tie he'd been expected to wear for Christmas evening at Sorrelton House, and into a comfortable pair of sweatpants and a faded and worn T-shirt. Then, leaning back against the headboard of his bed, he relaxed his shoulders for the first time in hours, and called Celeste.

'Hey.'

'Hey. You in bed?' She picked up far too quickly to be in company. Or maybe he just liked the idea of her in bed. Preferably his.

'Yeah.' A rustle of sheets as she stretched out. He could imagine her there, in the bed they'd shared the night before. He liked that he could picture it perfectly. That he could see her in his mind, if not in reality.

Careful, Theo.

He was treading a line here, one he'd been teetering on for so long he'd almost stopped noticing it. It would be oh-so-easy to slide over to the other side.

Except he had a feeling that the line might actually be a cliff edge, and he didn't want to fall.

Theo pushed away the thought that it could already be too late.

'How was your Christmas Day?' he asked, settling himself down more comfortably against the pillows.

'It started with a family intervention about my sex life, but after the fourth Bucks Fizz things started to improve. How was yours?'

'My parents hustled me up a rich and recently

dumped date for the occasion. She cried every time she saw the mistletoe they'd hung around the place.'

'Ouch.' He could picture her wincing, but also trying not to laugh. 'They hated me that much, huh?'

She was so quick, his Celeste. 'Apparently so.'

'Well, the good news is, my parents hate the idea of you just as much. Apparently, you're going to ruin my career prospects.'

'Probably true,' Theo admitted. 'You start hanging around with a lightweight like me for too long, they'll assume your brains have rotted out your ears.'

'Hey,' she said softly. It was a voice, a tone he'd not heard from her before. Gentle. Caring. 'Don't say that.'

He could get used to that voice.

'How are the happy couple?' he asked, shifting the conversation somewhere more comfortable. 'Did they at least get to celebrate in slightly more style than when they woke us up?'

'They're worried you're going to break my heart.' The mocking edge to her words told Theo exactly how ridiculous she thought that was. 'I reminded them that we had an agreement, and that this was all for show anyway.'

'Exactly,' Theo said, pushing away the part of his brain that had just been hoping for more.

'I mean, we could probably stop it now, if you wanted. Can't imagine anyone is going to be paying much attention to us over the festive period anyway, and we've kind of achieved what we set out to do.' Except then he'd never get to see her face as he told her how he'd stood up to his parents. Never get to see that small smile as she nodded and told him he'd done the right thing.

'The world no longer thinks you're a hideous, mansplaining arse-wipe,' Celeste said eloquently.

'And the TV-viewing public knows who you are, now,' he replied. 'So we're kind of done.'

'Yeah. I guess we are.'

The pause that followed was just about long enough to give him a tiny bit of hope back. Enough to say, 'Of course, if you wanted a last opportunity to laugh at me, I'm doing a freezing cold Boxing Day river swim in Henley tomorrow morning. I could pick you up on my way, if you wanted. Regale you with my Christmas Day recap—including a last-minute showdown with my father in which his face turned a shade of magenta not found in nature.'

It was, of course, completely out of his way, but he didn't feel like mentioning that.

'A wild swim?' Celeste laughed. 'Yeah, okay. I'd like to watch that. And hear about your showdown. Although I think nature really does have most shades of magenta, you know.'

He ignored that last bit, still smiling about the first. 'And then I'm supposed to be showing my face at some cocktails in igloos thing on Sunday,' he added.

'I've never had cocktails in an igloo before.'

'Apparently it's something everyone should try at least once in their lives.' Theo wondered if she knew how much he was making it up as he went along now. Talking absolute rubbish just for the excuse of seeing her again.

Probably. She was the smartest woman—smartest person—he'd ever met. She knew. And she was letting him get away with it. Why?

Maybe because she wants to spend more time with me, too. He hoped so anyway.

'Then how could I pass it up?' she said, laughing. 'Pick me up in the morning, and we can discuss whether swimming in the freezing cold Thames in December is better or worse than Christmas with our families.'

CHAPTER ELEVEN

It was still dark when Theo picked her up from her parents' town house the next morning. They'd barely got off the phone six hours earlier, so she hadn't had time to go home to her flat for fresh clothes, but fortunately her personal uniform of black, black and more black made it easy enough for her to dress from the stash she'd left in her childhood bedroom when she moved out, and still not look out of place.

'Why are you doing this, again?' Celeste settled into the passenger seat of Theo's sports car, while he dumped her bag in the back.

'Same reason I end up doing most things that seem like a bad idea at the time,' he replied, starting the engine.

'Publicity,' they both said, at once.

'Are you comparing sleeping with me to swimming in the freezing-cold Thames?' She shifted sideways in her seat as he pulled away from the kerb. The position had two advantages:

one, she could watch him better, and two, she could curl up here and get some more sleep while he drove.

'I'm comparing dating you in public to the Boxing Day Swim,' he corrected her. 'Sleeping with you was an added bonus.'

'I'm glad to hear it. And I want to hear about your showdown with your father, too.' Celeste yawned.

'Later,' Theo said. 'Get some more sleep for now.'

'Okay.' Her eyes fluttered shut as the motor purred, lulling her back to sleep.

When she awoke again, the built-up streets and buildings of London had given way to a gentler countryside—although Celeste knew they weren't far from the city centre, really.

Henley-on-Thames was only an hour's drive from London, and, given the early hour and the bank holiday emptiness of the roads in the pre-dawn, Celeste was pretty sure Theo had made it in considerably less. The Oxfordshire market town was famous for its Royal Regatta in the summer, which she could imagine Theo having to attend as part of his social obligations. It seemed *just* the sort of thing his parents would want to be seen at.

Somehow, a wild swim on a December morning seemed much more Theo-like, to her.

She hoped that his conversation with his parents would help him find more things that were more Theo-like, too. She liked Theo-like. And she was definitely still too tired to think properly if that was an actual sentence in her head.

Theo parked the car and they headed out together to find the other swimmers. There were more of them than Celeste had imagined would think this could possibly be a good idea, all lined up in swimsuits and blue-tinged skin.

'You don't even get to wear a wetsuit?' she asked Theo, incredulously.

'Apparently not.'

'There you are!' A young guy in a thick fleece coat hurried over to them, pushing through the crowd of warmly dressed bystanders who'd come to watch the spectacle. 'I was starting to think you weren't going to make it. Now, the camera crew is standing by to film the whole thing, but they'd like to get a quick chat with you before *and* after the swim, okay?'

Theo nodded. 'Fine. Remind me, how far am I swimming, Gaz?'

'Just seventy metres or so,' Gaz said. Celeste shivered in sympathy. 'From the hotel over there to some club down river, where they'll fish you out. The camera guys are going to follow you in the boat.'

'Great.' Theo looked as if he was starting

to seriously reconsider his life choices. Celeste didn't blame him.

'I'll get you some coffee ready at the other end?' she suggested.

Gaz had other ideas. 'We definitely want to get some footage of you cheering on your man too, Celeste. And a kiss at the end would go down a treat, yeah?'

He turned away, heading back to where the camera guys were waiting, leaving Theo and Celeste alone for a moment, before the insanity of the Boxing Day swim started.

'Guess I'm still a publicity asset after all,' Celeste said, unable not to watch as Theo stripped down to his swimming shorts. *God, he looks cold.*

'Guess so.' He flashed her one of those TV smiles. How he could smile like that, half naked in the frost, she had no idea. Must be level one TV training, or something.

It occurred to her, not for the first time, that she might never actually know what Theo was thinking. He was so good at hiding it all behind that made-for-TV facade of his. She'd pegged him as a faker their first lunch together, but knowing he was faking was only part of it. Being completely certain when he *wasn't* was much harder.

How much of their fake relationship was really fake and how much was really real? And how could she ever be sure?

The dark thought clouded her tired brain, and she couldn't seem to shake it away. So she tried a little fakery of her own, instead.

'Well, I'll have your coffee *and* your kiss waiting for you, then,' she said brightly. Then, pressing a swift kiss to his cheek, she headed off down the bank to where the other spectators were gathering to watch the swimmers set off.

'I don't think I'm ever going to be properly warm again,' Theo lamented, several hours later, as they headed back towards London in his convertible, heating on full.

'Well, if you hadn't fallen back in, after you got out in the first place, you might have warmed up sooner,' Celeste said, unhelpfully.

He shot her a glare. 'If you hadn't been doubled over with laughter, you might have helped me out.'

'I'd have spilt the coffee,' she countered.

Theo shook his head. All he knew was that there were going to be photos of him floundering around in the water like a drunken duck, and his supposed girlfriend laughing uproariously at him, all over the Internet by teatime. So much for regaining his dignity yesterday, by finally standing up to his parents. At least he didn't have to deal with what his father might have to say about the whole debacle debasing the family name any more.

'Want me to see if the photos have hit the Internet yet?' Celeste asked, reading his mind, as always.

He sighed. 'Might as well, I suppose. I'm sure they've been on social media for ages. See if they've hit the news pages yet, though.'

Her winces as she scrolled through her phone told him everything he needed to know.

Well, so he looked like an idiot. Again. It was all people really expected of him anyway. He was that nice but dim TV presenter, the un-threatening boy next door, the safe crush for teenage girls and grandmas alike.

Pretending to date Celeste might have actu-ally given him some intellectual and personal cache for once, but nobody expected it to last. Least of all him.

He knew his place in the world up to now. A rich kid without *quite* enough money, an aris-tocrat without *quite* enough connections, an av-erage learner with a wasted education, one he couldn't even quite see through. The only thing that would impress his parents was if he married someone who'd bolster the family finances and/ or social credibility—which he'd now told them he had no desire to do. And even if he had gone along with their plans, he was sure that within the year his mother would have been bemoaning the fact that he could have done better, and his father would be accusing him of not trying hard enough.

But where had trying hard ever got him, really?

It got you Celeste.

Not for long.

The victorious feeling he'd felt after standing up to his parents was already draining away like the freezing water he'd swum in. He'd closed one door, but had he really opened another? Yes, he wanted to go his own way, do his own thing. He just wasn't entirely sure what that way, or thing, was. Other than finishing his degree at last, and carrying on with work as always, what would really change?

'How bad is it?' Even humiliating photos had to be better than this train of thought. He could laugh them off, the same way he laughed off every insult and barb from his parents over the years, every time he was told he wasn't good enough. Every person who walked away when they realised that he wasn't quite enough of anything, after all.

'I mean… *I* think the way you're floundering around on the bank is quite endearing, really. Possibly.'

Theo smiled. From Celeste, that was positively a compliment. At least she was trying to make it less awful for him. She wouldn't have bothered to do that when they first met.

'So, hilariously humiliating, then?'

She nodded. 'Definitely going to be the funny story at the end of the news tonight, sorry.'

Theo sighed. He expected nothing less, really.

'Wait, though…'

He glanced across at Celeste and found her frowning at her phone. 'What?'

'There's a link to another article from this morning… Hang on…'

Maybe the bad feeling rising in his stomach had to do with how much of the River Thames he'd swallowed that morning.

But maybe not.

'What is it?' he asked, when she didn't say anything.

'Shhh. I'm reading.'

There was a junction coming up, and Theo took it, swinging off the motorway and into the forecourt of a service station. 'Show me,' he said, parking the car.

Silently, Celeste handed the phone over. Well, that wasn't good for a start. Celeste was seldom without something to say on a subject.

Theo scanned the article on her phone. Oh. Well, he didn't blame her.

'This was from when you took me to the Cressingham Arcade, before Christmas?' he guessed.

Celeste nodded. 'Must have been. Don't know why we didn't see it before now, but I suppose it's only been a few days.'

They'd been shopping for a present suitable for his mother, since he'd left it to the last minute as usual. Celeste had suggested the arcade where her brother and Rachel were working, so they'd popped there after one of their regular 'out to be seen' lunches together.

And apparently someone had snapped a photo of them supposedly looking at engagement rings at the grumpy old jeweller's shop.

Following the links in the article, he traced the story back to its original source—a tweet posted by a random member of the public, four days ago. 'Looks like it was just some normal person posting it, and they misspelt the hashtag, so it took a while for the gossip sites to pick it up.'

'So, the world thinks we're getting married? Our parents are going to hate that.'

Theo chuckled. 'They definitely are.'

'Good thing it's not true, then.'

And it was. A good thing. Because he wasn't looking to settle down and get married, not even just to prove a point to his parents. And if he were… He and Celeste were from different worlds, different expectations, and different ambitions. He was populist, she was highbrow. He was lightweight, she was a walking history textbook.

She'd be bored of him in no time, and he was sure he'd be a disappointment to her the same way he'd always been to his parents.

Except…if his parents were wrong, if he'd stepped out of that toxic family circle and accepted that maybe there was more to him than they saw…what if Celeste could see that too?

As he pulled back onto the motorway, he couldn't help but let a little hope bubble up inside him.

Theo dropped her back at her own flat, and for the first time since Christmas Eve Celeste finally had space to think. To figure out what the hell was going on in her head—and in her heart.

The rest of the journey back from Henley-on-Thames had been mostly silent. And knowing how badly Theo had needed a shower and a sleep, she hadn't even considered inviting him up to the flat with her.

But now she was there, alone with her thoughts, she almost wished she had. If nothing else, Theo was always a pleasant distraction.

Except he was so much more than that. That was the problem.

They needed to talk. They'd gone into this as a fun scheme, a trick to play on social media, almost. A way to rehabilitate Theo's reputation after Celeste's performance on the *Christmas Cracker Cranium Quiz*, and to raise her profile ahead of her potential TV show.

A TV show she'd heard nothing but warnings from her parents about all Christmas Day, even after she'd told them she didn't want to talk about it, to the point where she was starting to wonder if they might even be right. Oh, not about the need to share history with anyone willing to learn it; she still believed that. But was she really the right person to do it? Was she choosing a career in media as a mediocre historian over her academic focus? All her life, she'd followed the path laid out for her by her parents, but now she was standing at a fork in that road, and choosing the one they'd put 'do not cross' tape over.

And that led her right back to Theo.

She and her agent had pitched the show before she'd met Theo, of course, but back then it was just a concept, a possibility. Now, her agent was emailing daily with updates instead of monthly. Apparently, her raised media profile had everyone keen to get moving with the project, and it looked more like a sure thing every day. And while she'd planned to be mostly consulting and narrating, now they wanted her front and centre on camera.

They'd even changed the title of the show to include her name. Suddenly, it was more about her than the history, than the stories of ancient women she wanted to tell.

She wasn't an idiot. She knew all of that was because of Theo, not her. But what would happen when Theo wasn't part of her life—or her image—any more?

Because he wouldn't be.

They hadn't expressly discussed breaking up, but the plan had never been a long-term one. They lived in different worlds, for all that she might be inhabiting his for a little while. She had research to do, a book to finish, a name to make for herself in her chosen niche.

The TV show was one project, one year. What about the rest of her life?

Theo had talked about what might happen next for her over dinner one night, while they had both studiously avoiding looking at the guy seated at the next table taking their photo.

'You've got your foot in the door now, and that's all it takes,' he'd said, while feeding her one of the prawns from his starter. 'Radio appearances was one thing, but once you're on TV once, that's it. You'll be the channel's go-to expert on all things historical.'

'But I'm *not* an expert on all things historical,' she'd pointed out. 'I have a speciality. *That's* what I'm an expert in.'

'You know more general history than almost everyone else in the population,' he'd countered. 'That's what matters. They'll rope you in for all sorts of historical programmes now—look at that guy who does all the science stuff. What's his name? He's a physicist, but he ends up on shows about all sorts.'

He was right, Celeste knew now. Her area of expertise was women's history, especially women in the ancient world. But already she'd found herself approached to talk on other topics. Topics that fascinated her, sure, but they weren't her niche. They weren't what she was supposed to be talking about.

Like the history of Christmas. She'd spent a week reading up on that before the quiz show, and look where that landed her. At dire risk of falling for a guy who was only in it for the publicity. And who would always belong to a world she wasn't sure she wanted to be a part of.

She pulled her phone back out to look again at the photo of her and Theo at the jeweller's shop. They hadn't been looking at rings, of course.

But some strange emotion tugging at her heart kept whispering, *What if you had?*

Stop it. She wasn't going down that road.

She swiped out of the browser and checked her message and email notifications instead.

Eight messages. Two from Rachel, one linking her to the article about the jeweller's and asking if there was something she needed to tell her, and one with a link to a navy bridesmaid's dress with the word Compromise? underneath. One from Damon that was just a picture of Theo falling in the water at the wild swim and a lot of laughing emojis.

Two from her mother, obliquely mentioning Theo's existence and her disapproval of it, and another one from her father doing the same but without any of the subtlety.

One from her agent, with a thumbs-up emoji next to a photo of her and Theo, and a note about a meeting with the production company first thing in the new year.

And one from Theo, of course.

Igloo cocktails tomorrow. I'll pick you up at eight.
x

CHAPTER TWELVE

IGLOOS ON A roof terrace in a city centre, with integral champagne bars.

'Only in London,' Theo observed as they stood outside their own private igloo and took in the city skyline.

The igloos themselves had a large window built in—or left open, really—to enjoy the views, but since Theo had a feeling it would be even colder in there than outside, he was putting it off for the moment. He still hadn't fully warmed up since his dip in the Thames, and even the fake fur coats provided by the owners of the establishment weren't doing much except make him feel like an extra in *Game of Thrones*.

'Mmm,' Celeste agreed absently as she leaned against the railings to look out.

She'd seemed mostly absent since he picked her up. As if her body was present, but her mind had gone wandering. When he'd asked her about it, she'd muttered something about her book, and research, and thinking through ideas.

He was glad she was able to think about work. Because the only thing *he'd* been able to think about for days now was her.

Whatever this thing between them had morphed into, it wasn't what they'd agreed at the start. Which meant they had to talk about what happened next. And that meant talking about what had happened on Christmas Eve, too—and if she wanted it to happen again.

Theo had done a lot of thinking the day before, once he'd warmed up enough for proper thoughts, but he wasn't sure he'd come to any sensible conclusions. Despite it being Boxing Day, and a bank holiday, his agent Cerys had been on the phone the moment she'd seen the pictures of them at the jeweller's shop in the arcade, asking what was going on.

'I told you that you could call it off,' she'd said, sounding amused. 'Do I take this to mean you're heading in a rather different direction?'

'It wasn't what it looked like,' Theo had told her tiredly. 'But…but if it was, would it be so bad?'

Cerys had paused at that, and when she'd spoken again, he'd been able to hear the surprise in her voice. 'Well, I guess that depends on your perspective. I mean, getting married to anyone would kind of dampen your crush appeal a little bit, and I'm guessing you wouldn't want to court social media by appearing in public with up-and-coming celebrities on your arm any more, so there's that. But stars settle down and it doesn't ruin their careers or anything, if that's what you mean. But really, Theo…her? Are you sure? She decimated you on that quiz show. To be honest, I thought there was solid chance she'd do worse than throw coffee over you on that first date.'

'She doesn't like it when history doesn't tell the truth,' Theo had replied, automatically. 'And the answers on those cards were wrong. Well, incomplete, at least.'

Cerys had laughed at that. 'Well, that tells me everything I need to know. You've got it bad. Good luck with that, then.' And she'd hung up.

Theo had wanted to call back, to tell her that Celeste wasn't the person people seemed to think. That, maybe, neither was he.

Because when he was with Celeste, he believed that there was more to him than he'd ever been led to believe. More than just a rich kid with every advantage who still couldn't be anything more than a nice smile and a winning personality.

Something more than just the Montgomery

name, as his parents believed, or his face, as the viewing public seemed to think.

The question was, did she feel the same way when she was with him? Or, as he feared, did she think he made her less?

Unfortunately, there was only one way to find out. And that meant having a conversation he wasn't at all sure he wanted to have.

The one about what happened next.

He waited until they both had fresh drinks, and had taken their icy seats inside the igloo. Celeste still seemed a little as if she were on another planet, but she smiled at least as he handed her an extra blanket, laying it out across both of them as they looked out of the cut-out window.

'If I interrupt your thinking will you throw a drink at me?' Theo figured it was best to start with the basics and work up.

Celeste turned to him with a smirk hovering around her lips. 'You're tempting fate just asking, you realise?'

'I know.'

She sipped at her drink. 'But luckily for you this cocktail is too delicious for me to waste it on you. And I'm being a terrible fake date, right? Sorry. Am I supposed to be fawning over you more?'

'No one is looking,' Theo said. It felt weirdly uncomfortable to hear her talk about them that way, after everything. 'And besides, I think we're past all that now, aren't we?'

'*Are* we?' Celeste asked. 'Have you seen the photos from the Boxing Day swim? Whoever is in charge of social media over at your channel has been having a grand old time showcasing our relationship right alongside the listings for your New Year's Eve show.'

'That's just coincidence. And that's not about us anyway.'

'Except it is, right?' Celeste pressed. 'I mean, right from the start that's exactly what we were about. Putting forward the right image for you—and for me too, I guess.'

He didn't like where this was going. Something was twisting in his gut, and he didn't think it was the cocktails.

'At the start, sure. But after Christmas Eve—'

She interrupted him with a laugh, high and tinkling, one that barely sounded like Celeste at all.

He was missing something here. She hadn't been like this at Henley, had she? What had changed since yesterday?

The photo of them at the jeweller's. Was that what was bothering her?

'Is this about the photos yesterday? The stories about us getting engaged?'

'Why would it be about them?' She looked

down into her glass as she spoke, and Theo knew she was avoiding his gaze. He was right, even if she wasn't going to admit it. 'They were just stupid stories. We know it's not like that between us.'

'Right.' Except… 'Why isn't it?'

Her shocked gaze met his in an instant. 'What do you mean?'

Theo took a breath. This was it. His chance.

He wanted this feeling to last—the feeling he had when he was with Celeste. Which meant being honest with her. Being real. No TV charm and smile, no spin for social media. No faking.

Just him. And her.

'Why isn't it that way between us? I mean, not getting married exactly, but…we've had fun, right? Together? We could keep having fun, maybe?'

No.

She'd thought she could read him, but she'd never seen this coming. She'd known he was a faker, but she'd never though he'd take it this far.

She'd thought she'd known what she was doing, but now she was pretty sure she had no idea at all.

'I think we should break up. Fake break up. Send a press release, whatever it is we need to do to end this.' Celeste started to stand up, pushing the blanket away from her lap, before she realised she was about to bang her head on the rounded ceiling of the igloo, and sat back down.

She wanted to get away, but she didn't want an audience for this, either. So apparently, she was having the most important conversation of her life so far that didn't take place in front of an academic board in an igloo. Because that was the sort of thing that happened when a person hung around with Theo Montgomery for too long.

'You think… Why?' He shook his head as he looked at her. 'You can't tell me we're not good together. Christmas Eve—'

'Was lovely,' she interrupted him again. The only way she was going to get through this was by not letting him talk too much. That silver tongue of his could probably talk her into anything; wasn't that how she'd ended up in this mess to begin with?

'So what's the problem here, exactly?' Theo asked.

'You and me…it's been fun,' she admitted. 'But it hasn't been real, we both know that. Hell, that was what we agreed! It was all for show. And yes, I'm attracted to you, yes, I had fun with you—'

'Then why—?'

'But that doesn't change the basic facts of this situation,' she shouted over him.

'And those facts are?' His voice was calmer than she thought she'd ever heard it before. He almost didn't sound like himself. Everything about him was always so alive, so full of fun and mischief. But right now he sounded as dry as her last boyfriend, the philosophy student.

As if this wasn't an act at all.

Don't think about that.

'We come from different worlds,' she said slowly. 'Yes, I'm dabbling in TV, but I've spent my whole life building up my academic career.'

'And you think that continuing to be seen with me would undermine your credentials. I'd make you look lightweight.'

'No! That wasn't what I—'

'Wasn't it?' His mouth twisted in an unfriendly smile. 'Or is it worse than that? You've had your fun with me, but I'm not an intellectual match for you, right? You were slumming it with the stupid TV star for a while, having fun looking at my little history essays for my meaningless bachelor's degree, but I'm never going to live up to those professors you meet at conferences, or whatever.'

'You're not stupid,' Celeste said quietly. 'I never said—or thought—you were stupid.'

'Didn't you?' Theo shook his head. 'Then you

must have been the first. If you think I don't know what people say about me—' He broke off.

'Look, it's not you,' she said desperately. 'It's me. And, God, I know that's the most overused line in break-up history, but really. Think about it. I'm grumpy and hyper-focussed, I have no ability to connect with people, really. I can't help but tell them when they're wrong. Your parents hate me—'

'Yours hate me, too.'

'True. And maybe…maybe they're right.'

'To hate me?' Theo's eyebrows went up at that.

'No! They think…they think that your lifestyle, your fame, would distract me from my studies. It would lead me away from academia into the sort of history lite you see in bad documentaries on TV. Like you said, the producers don't care about my area of expertise—history is just history to them. I wouldn't be taken seriously as an academic any more.'

'You might have a lot more fun, though,' Theo pointed out quietly. 'You *love* history, Celeste. Not just certain parts of it—all of it. Is it really so important to you to be an expert in one thing, rather than good at lots of it? More than sharing it with the world?'

'Yes.' Because it always had been. That had

been the message from her parents from her earliest days. Find what you're passionate about and pursue it with everything you have. Don't look left or right, don't get distracted. Find what matters to you and make yourself matter.

Damon had gone the other way entirely, but she…she'd embraced the philosophy. She'd gone after academia, a professorship, as her ultimate goal. Working to publish her academic tome on women in history, to prove her place in the canon. And if she gave it up now…what did that leave her?

She'd only ever been good at talking to other academics. If she tried to teach the Great British Public about history instead…would they even listen?

What if she was just wasting her time?

This wasn't one fun quiz show where she was a novelty, a festive amusement. And it wasn't being seen around town with Theo, a curiosity. This was trying to be the real thing, and make people listen to her—when the only person outside academia and Rachel who'd ever done that was Theo, and she didn't even know for sure that he wasn't just faking it.

The university was safer. She knew the rules there, had been training for it all her life.

Life with Theo was the opposite of safe. It was people watching her, commenting on her all the time. It was expanding her secure little bubble so much further outside the university than she'd planned.

This wasn't a one-off TV show. This was a career change—a life change—she wasn't sure she was ready for.

Theo's jaw was clenched, as if he was holding in all the words he wanted to say. He always did, she realised suddenly, surprised that she knew such a detail about him. But this was how he'd been at lunch with his parents, too. Biting his tongue, holding in everything he was thinking.

Was that just how he'd been brought up? Or was it part of who he was now? All the years smiling for the cameras, being the nice guy... hell, he'd only fake dated her in the first place to preserve that image.

But Celeste wanted to hear what he *really* thought, not what he believed he *should* think.

He'd said it to his parents on Christmas Day, by all accounts. How much had that taken out of him? To finally speak up to them?

It didn't look as if he was going to do the same for her, though.

He threw down the rest of his cocktail, swallowing it fast, and slamming his glass onto the ice table. Getting to his feet, his head still bowed to avoid hitting it on the ceiling, he gave her an awkward nod. 'Do you need me to take you home?'

'Theo…' She trailed off. What could she say? He'd asked for something she wasn't ready or able to give. How could she now ask him to stay?

She shook her head. 'I'm fine.'

'In that case… I'll see you around, Celeste.' He turned and walked out, leaving her alone in the icy shelter.

She wished her heart were as frozen as the igloo. Then maybe it wouldn't hurt so much.

'Are you sure you're okay to do this?' Cerys asked as Theo had his mic checked for what was hopefully the last time.

'Of course, I'm okay. Why wouldn't I be?' He wasn't even sure what his agent was *doing* here for the *New Year's Eve Spectacular*. She didn't normally come to his filming, but maybe she had nowhere else to be for the biggest party night of the calendar.

Although he supposed he was sort of *hosting* the biggest party on that biggest party night. Other people probably really wanted to be there. Even if he was wishing he were anywhere but.

'Because you've been—how can I put this?— not your charming self over the last few days.'

Days filled with last-minute meetings and planning, and absolutely no Celeste. Except for the photos of her, which were still all over social media, and people asking him about her.

There was even one photo of her leaving the igloo bar, after him. He'd been staring at it for days now trying to figure out if her eyes in it were red from crying or the cold.

Probably the cold. This was Celeste, after all.

As she'd told him, she didn't really *do* people. At least, not ones who weren't dead and were without an interesting backstory or place in history.

He'd known. He'd known from the start that he couldn't fit into her world, that she'd be another person he wasn't good enough for. And yet he'd let himself hope…

She was the one person who'd made him believe he was more than his name or his face, more than his TV-star status, and more than his parents told him he could be.

It just turned out *she* didn't believe it.

'And now you look like you're trying to burn down the Tower of London with lasers from your eyes,' Cerys went on. 'Is this about Celeste?'

He spun away from the Tower to face her. 'Why would it be about Celeste?' And who the hell decided to do the filming here, where he had to look at that place—the place he'd kissed her properly for the first time—all night long?

Probably him, in one of those meetings he hadn't been paying attention in.

'Because you haven't been seen with her in days, you haven't mentioned her name once until now, and you've practically growled at anyone who mentions it to you.' Cerys was not a touchy-feely, reassuring agent. The fact that she felt the need to pat Theo's arm gently was a definite warning sign that he was losing it completely. 'What happened, Theo?'

'We ended it,' he said, with a shrug.

She ripped half my heart out with an ice pick, froze it and used it to cool her cocktail.

'It was all very mutual and friendly. After all, we were never *really* together in the first place, remember.'

Even if it felt like we were. Even if it felt like everything.

'Right.' Cerys did not look in any way convinced. 'Did you tell her?'

'Tell her what?' he asked, confused.

'That you're in love with her.'

He had enough practice at looking amused when he wasn't from listening to the poor jokes told on various shows he'd hosted, but it still took everything in his power to laugh at Cerys's words, when what was left of his heart felt as if it were trying to break out of his body.

'Why on earth would I tell her that?' he scoffed.

Cerys rolled her eyes and patted his arm again. 'Just get through tonight, yeah? Then we can go get really drunk and you can cry on my shoulder for a while, and in the morning it'll be a brand-new year and you can move on. Well, after the hangover subsides.'

He waited until she'd moved out of his line of sight to let his amused smile drop.

Oh, God, he was in love with Celeste Hunter. How the hell had that happened?

The worst part was, he knew *exactly* how and when it had happened, and he hadn't done anything to stop it.

No. The worst part was that she didn't love him back.

But the *second*-to-worst part…he'd fallen for her the moment she'd scowled at him, maybe. Or when she'd thrown coffee over his lap. Or when she'd sat in a hot tub on a boat and looked so adorably baffled by the whole experience. Or when he'd kissed her on the ice rink across the river at the Tower. Or when she'd sat through a hideous dinner with his parents. Or when she'd talked to him about history and expected him to keep up. Or when she'd told him he was nothing like the man his parents thought he was. Or when she'd kissed him in the hallway and taken him to bed. Or when she'd pulled him out of the river, or when she'd sat with him in an igloo...

The truth was, he hadn't fallen for her once. It hadn't been love at first sight. It had been love, inch by inch. With every story about a ghost bear or the truth about Christmas trees. He'd been fascinated from the start, but the love... that had crept in, without him even knowing it was there.

Until it was so much a part of his heart he thought it might stop beating without it.

God, he was pathetic.

But he didn't have time to dwell on that right now. He had a show to present, and a cheery persona to find again. Cerys was right: he could mope once the work was done, and not before.

Turning his back firmly on the Tower of London, Theo took a deep breath, turned to the anxious-looking production assistant hovering nearby, and said, 'I'm ready.'

CHAPTER THIRTEEN

'WHERE HAVE YOU BEEN?' Rachel asked as Celeste eased her way through the crowds of people at the Cressingham Arcade, all there to celebrate her brother and best friend's engagement, and the new year, not necessarily in that order.

'Sorry, I got caught up writing, lost track of time,' Celeste lied. Well, sort of lied. The losing track of time part was real. The writing, less so.

Seemed as though ever since she'd let Theo walk away so she could focus on her academic writing, she'd written less than ever.

Rachel gave her the sort of look that told her she wasn't buying it at all, then led her over to where the bar was situated, at the back of the arcade. Right next to the jeweller's shop, where she'd been photographed with Theo.

That was the real reason she was late. She hadn't wanted to come. Damon had bought her a T-shirt with that on it one year: 'Sorry I'm late, I didn't want to come.' She should have worn it tonight.

She'd only been here with Theo for an hour or so, and yet it was already filled with memories of him. Her parents' house was unbearable, and she wasn't letting herself anywhere near the Tower of London.

She wanted to stay safe, locked away in her office, where there were no memories of Theo to distract her.

Rachel shoved a champagne flute into her hand. 'Okay, time to talk. What's going on? It's to do with Theo, I take it?'

Celeste looked at her best friend—newly engaged, madly in love, with newfound confidence at work and in herself—and burst into tears.

'Right. This way, then.' Rachel bundled her towards a door, hidden away in the wall between two tiled pillars, and pushed her through it. Together, they climbed a metal staircase to a balcony Celeste hadn't ever even noticed from the ground floor.

Sitting with their backs against the door, champagne glasses in hand, the two best friends looked up at the painted ceiling of the Victorian shopping arcade.

'What do you see?' Rachel asked.

Celeste blinked as the ceiling came into focus. 'Butterflies!'

Dozens of tiny painted butterflies, so realistic she almost thought one might flutter down and land on her outstretched finger.

'Damon brought me up here, the first time I visited the arcade,' Rachel said. 'He showed me so many secret things about the place. But that's not why I fell in love with him.'

'Why *did* you fall in love with him?' As much as Celeste loved her brother, she wasn't sure he was an automatic catch for any woman, and she still thought he'd probably got the far better end of the bargain in marrying Rachel.

'Because he showed me the secret places inside me, too,' Rachel said.

Celeste pulled a face. 'If this is a sex thing, I really don't want to hear it. That's my brother, remember, and I'm having a hard enough time this week as it is.'

Rachel laughed, the sound ringing off the metal railings. 'That's not what I meant! I mean…he showed me who I could be, if I let myself. If I believed in myself, even—believed it was possible, and went after it.'

'And here I was thinking *you* were the one who showed him he could fall in love, and stop jumping from one thing to the next,' Celeste replied, bumping her shoulder against her best friend's.

'Maybe that's the point,' Rachel mused. 'We both changed—or rather, we both found the parts of ourselves we'd stopped believing in, over the years.'

'That sounds nice.'

'It is,' Rachel agreed. 'So, what did Theo teach *you* about yourself?'

'What do you mean?' Celeste started at the question, and Rachel rolled her eyes.

'Come on, it's obvious that you've fallen for him. You're madly in love and, to be honest, I think that was kind of inevitable from the start.'

'Coming from someone who tried to claim that she was having nothing but a "festive fling" and ended up engaged before Christmas morning,' Celeste grumbled.

'So I know what I'm talking about.' Sighing, Rachel rested her head against Celeste's shoulder. 'It's just me, Celeste. Tell me everything.'

Celeste took one last look up at the butterflies, free and wild and unreal on the ceiling, and started talking.

She told her about the kiss on the ice rink, about the way Theo actually listened when she talked about weird historical facts, and didn't mind—even liked it—when she corrected those things that everyone thought they knew. She talked about how his parents hated her, and hers hated him, and how she didn't care. Because her parents only cared about her career, and his parents only cared about their name and their money, so why should either of them care what they thought anyway? And she talked about Christmas Eve, and the wild swim and the jeweller's photos and then she talked about the igloos…

'Why?' Rachel asked. 'Why did you tell him that your academic career was more important than what's between you? I know you better than that, Celeste, even if he doesn't, yet. You're not your parents, even if you think you are. So why?'

'You're not your parents.'

She wasn't sure if she'd ever realised how much she needed someone to say those words to her.

'Because… I was scared.' Rachel would know how much it cost her to admit it. She'd always powered through life, pretending she didn't care when people laughed at her, or rolled their eyes and walked away when she corrected them. 'He's not like me, Rach. People *like* him. He's friendly and nice and gorgeous and popular and—'

'And you didn't think you could have that?'

'I didn't think I could keep it. I still don't. I'm not good at people—everyone knows that about me. So I pretended it was all about work, and my academic reputation, because I didn't want to admit the truth. I'm in love with him and it would hurt like hell when he walked away from me like every other guy in my life has, when they realise that this is just me. I can't not tell them when they're wrong. I can't play nice with their parents. And I'm going to forget about important dinners and stuff if I'm reading something interesting.'

'Or abandon your brother and best friend at a party while you escape to the library,' Rachel added, mildly.

Celeste rolled her eyes. 'It was nine years ago, Rachel. Are you two ever going to forgive me for that?'

She grinned. 'I think we probably will. And I think Theo would too, if you asked him to.'

'If I admitted I was wrong?' That…did not sound like the sort of thing she would do.

'Is he worth it?'

'Yes.' The word was out before she could even think about it. 'But he was talking about a casual thing. We never said anything about love. And I don't think I could take it if—'

'Give him a chance,' Rachel suggested. 'You never told him you loved him, either, right?'

'No.'

'So tell him. Tell him you were wrong and that you love him.'

'And what if he says he doesn't love me back?'

Rachel gave her a sympathetic smile. 'Then you're no worse off than you are now. And at least you'll know, yeah?'

'I suppose.' It still sounded like a risky deal to her.

'Just…trust me, okay?' Rachel said. 'The people we love are worth taking a chance on. Even if it means admitting we're wrong, sometimes.'

'Damon taught you that too?'

'And you.' Rachel flashed her a grin. 'After all, it's hard to be best friends with you for a decade without admitting you're wrong a couple of hundred times.'

'Very true.' Celeste got to her feet, saying a silent goodbye to the butterflies. 'So, this is your engagement party. I'm guessing a good maid of honour would stay until the end?'

'As long as you promise me you're going to find Theo and not run off to the library, I'll cover for you.'

Grinning, Celeste pressed a quick kiss to her best friend's cheek and raced down the stairs.

It was almost a new year. And she had to do something very important before the clock chimed midnight.

He could feel the Tower of London looming behind him, reminding him of everything he was leaving behind in the old year.

Even as midnight approached, and the crowd of revellers along the banks of the Thames grew louder, and more excitable, Theo couldn't get himself in the right mood. Oh, he pasted on the work smile and played the part, but inside, he was thinking. Hard.

While the band of the moment played their last song before the midnight countdown, he used the break to marshal his thoughts into an order—or rather a list.

New Year's Resolutions.
One: Finish my history degree.

He'd been working on it part-time for years now, and it was time to wrap it up. Not least because he knew, deep down, he'd only been putting it off because he still didn't feel he deserved it.

Well, sod that. He'd done the work—or most of it anyway. Even Celeste had said it was good. So he'd finish the rest. He'd earned it. It might not be an Oxbridge first, but it was something he'd worked for himself, without any extra credit for his name or his face, and that made it all the more valuable to Theo.

Two: Figure out what I want to do next.

He'd told his parents it wouldn't be what they wanted. Maybe he needed to say the same thing to the TV studios. Take a break, and figure out what it was that he wanted to achieve. To do something for himself, for a change. He'd made enough money from his TV career—probably even enough to save a money pit like the family home if he wanted to, which he didn't. He could afford to take a break, a step back at least, while he got his head straight.

His whole life, he'd tried to make nice, to keep everyone on side, to earn *someone's* approval at least. Hell, even fake dating Celeste had been about winning back public approval, to start with. And where had that desperate need to be liked got him?

Well, actually, it had got him pretty far in his career, he thought, looking out over the crowd cheering the band up on stage. But in his personal life?

He supposed it had brought him to Celeste, but it hadn't been enough to let him keep her. And it had also brought him to the place where his parents thought it was okay to try and arrange a marriage for him to further their own ambitions.

That was not okay. And he'd told them so. He wanted to keep that feeling of freedom he'd experienced when he'd done it.

New Year, new Theo.

They'd called—well, his mother had, merrily whitewashing the whole of Christmas Day as if it had never happened. And normally he'd let her get away with it.

Not this time.

He'd go and see them again, as they'd asked. But he was standing firm, now. He'd tell them that he had his own life, his own career. That he was happy and successful. That if he ever married it would be because he loved the person, and it wouldn't matter to him what they thought of his choice. Because they'd never really been particularly pleased that *he* was their son. Never said they were proud of him, or that they loved him. Only ever pointed out his faults.

And he had no intention of letting them do that to his wife, or any children that might be in his future.

He'd put up with it his whole life, but that was no reason anyone else had to.

What else could he put on his list for his best year ever?

Three: Fall in love.

Except he'd already done that, hadn't he?

He shook the thought away. The band were coming to the end of the song, and he could feel the atmosphere rising around him as midnight drew closer.

This was why he loved his job; being around so many people at moments like this, connecting with them, helping them celebrate, feeling a part of it all.

He just wished Celeste were there to share it with him.

The last chord rang out across the crowd, rippling over the river, past the Tower of London behind him. The giant video screen they'd set up at the edge of the water switched from showing the band on stage, to showing him again—then split to show a live image of Big Ben, further down the river.

'It's nearly time, guys!' Theo yelled into his mic, earning a roar of excitement from the crowd in return. 'Are you ready to count down with me?' Another screaming affirmative.

He waited until he got the signal in his earpiece, pressing it into his ear and concentrating to make sure it didn't get lost in the noise of the party below.

'Ten!' he shouted, knowing from there on

he was almost obsolete. He'd given them their starting line, and from here the crowd would take the momentum he'd built and run with it.

Except there was something happening, just below where he stood on the stage. Something distracting the crowd from the most important countdown of the year.

'Nine,' he yelled, almost a millisecond too late, as he frowned down at the scene. What was happening down there?

'Eight!' There was someone pushing through the crowds.

'Seven!' Someone with dark hair.

'Six!' And a familiar white coat.

'Five!' And bright red lips as she smiled up at him.

Celeste.

He lost his place in the countdown for a second, as he tried to process the reality of her being there, now.

'Four!' he yelled, slightly behind the rest of the crowd. The people at the front of the crowd were helping her up onto the stage now. Everyone knew who she was, clearly. And who she was to him.

'Three!' She stood before him, eyes hopeful, biting her lip.

'I couldn't start the new year without you,' she shouted, the words hitting his heart.

'Two!' He hadn't moved. He needed to move, to respond, something.

Celeste took a step back, and he reached out to grab her hand and pull her close against his side, as the crowd screamed for them both.

'One!' He looked Celeste in the eye and hoped she could read in his face everything he couldn't say. At least, not without the crowd and millions of TV viewers hearing it too, through his microphone.

The confetti cannons went off, the balloons sailed down river, and Big Ben bonged to mark the end of one year and the start of another.

'Happy New Year!' Theo yelled, to the crowd, to the viewers, to Celeste and to himself.

And then he kissed her, in front of millions of people, and there wasn't anything fake about it at all.

Celeste fell into his kiss as if she'd been waiting aeons for it, not days. She didn't care who was watching, or what anybody thought. She just knew she was where she belonged. Standing in the shadow of the Tower of London, kissing the man she loved.

Oh. She should probably tell him that, shouldn't she?

'I love you,' she murmured between kisses.

'I love you, too,' he replied, just as an almighty crash tore through the air as the fireworks started. They turned to watch as the sky over the Tower was lit up with colours and patterns, and 'Auld Lang Syne' kicked in on the bagpipes over on the other stage.

'I'm sorry.' Now she was here, she felt the desperate need to tell him all the things she hadn't, that night in the igloo. 'I was a fool. I was scared.'

'Me, too,' Theo admitted. 'Think that maybe we could be scared together?'

She smiled up at him. 'If I'm with you, I don't think I'll have to be afraid.'

'Not ever,' he promised.

Celeste snuggled into his arms as the party continued below.

'How much longer are you hosting this shindig for?' she asked.

'We're live for another fifteen minutes. But after that… I'm all yours.'

'For ever?' It was a big ask. Too big. They still hadn't talked about all the reasons she'd pulled away, or why he'd let her. All the things that were holding them back from the lives they could be living, together.

'If you'll have me,' Theo replied, and she knew suddenly that none of it mattered.

Yes, they had plenty of stuff to work through, but it would all be easier with each other by their sides. They had a whole new year stretching out before them—a whole new life, even—in which to work out the details.

'Always,' she replied.

There was an anxious-looking production assistant waving at Theo from just off camera. Celeste waved back and pressed a quick kiss to Theo's cheek before starting to move away.

Theo grabbed her back and kissed her properly, on the lips. 'Don't go far.'

'Promise.'

She slid away, out of camera view, and watched as the live broadcast on the big screen lit up with Theo's face again. She hid her smile behind her hand as she realised he had her pillar-box red lipstick liberally smeared around his mouth. *Oops.*

'And that's it, folks!' Theo said finally, wrapping up the live broadcast. 'The old year has passed, the new one is here. No need to stop celebrating though! And I hope the rest of your night—the rest of your year, for that matter—is as incredible as I hope mine is going to be. Happy New Year, Britain!'

More cheering as the cameras panned out over the crowds, the river and the Tower of London again. Theo shook hands with a dozen or more people as he made his way towards her, but Celeste didn't mind the wait.

He was right. They had a whole year to make special—and, she hoped, a whole lifetime. Together.

Finally, he reached her side and took her hand in his. 'Ready?' he asked.

'For what?'

'Our future.'

Celeste smiled. 'Absolutely.' History was her first love, of course. But even it couldn't live up to the prospect of a future with the man she loved more than anything.

* * * * *

If you missed the previous story in the Cinderellas in the Spotlight duet, then check out

Awakening His Shy Cinderella

And if you enjoyed this story, check out these other great reads from Sophie Pembroke

Italian Escape with Her Fake Fiancé
Second Chance for the Single Mom
Snowbound with the Heir

All available now!